LUCY DANIELS

Animal Ark™

Pony Parade
Guinea-pig Gang
Gerbil Genius

D1353777

LUCY DANIELS

Pony
Parade

Hodder
Children's
Books

A division of Hachette Children's Books

This edition of Pony Parade, Guinea-pig Gang and Gerbil Genius
first published in 1999.

This edition published in 2008

ISBN-13: 978 0 340 95684 7

Pony Parade

Special thanks to Pat Posner

Text copyright © 1997 Working Partners Ltd.
Created by Working Partners Ltd, W6 0QT
Original series created by Ben M. Baglio
Illustrations copyright © 1997 Paul Howard
Cover illustration by Chris Chapman

First published as a single volume in Great Britain in 1997
by Hodder Children's Books

For more information about Animal Ark,
please contact www.animalark.co.uk

1

A Catalogue record for this book is available from the British Library

Typeset in Bembo by Avon DataSet Ltd,
Bidford-on-Avon, Warwickshire

Printed and bound in Great Britain by Clays Ltd, St Ives plc

The paper and board used in this paperback by Hodder Children's
Books are natural recyclable products made from wood grown in
sustainable forests. The manufacturing processes conform to the
environmental regulations of the country of origin.

Hodder Children's Books
a division of Hachette Children's Books
338 Euston Road, London NW1 3BH
An Hachette Livre UK company

Contents

Contents

1

James on holiday

"Come on, Blackie," Mandy said. She smiled down at the young Labrador and tugged gently on his lead. "We'll have to turn round and go back now. They'll be waiting for you!"

Blackie wagged his tail and carried on snuffling at the grass verge. "Come *on*!"

Mandy said more firmly. "You've sniffed enough to last for hours. Besides, here's James coming to fetch us," she added as she saw her best friend running down the lane.

"Hurry up, Mandy," James called. "We're almost ready to leave."

Blackie looked up at the sound of James's voice. Then, barking joyfully, he tugged Mandy off towards him.

"Well, *that* got him moving!" Mandy chuckled, handing Blackie's lead to James.

"Good job too," James said. "Mum and Dad are just loading the last lot of stuff into the car. Gosh, Mandy, there are so many bags. You'd think we were going for a month, not just three days!"

Just then Blackie started pulling at the lead and James groaned. "Not that way, Blackie. Back home quickly, boy. Dad won't want to be kept waiting. Oh, help!" he added. "Now he's wound his lead round my legs."

Mandy bent down to unwind the lead. As soon as she'd done it, Blackie jumped up at her and nearly knocked her over. "What a pest you are, Blackie," she said lovingly. "Now, get walking!"

"That's what he was like before you came and took him out," James said as, at last, Blackie started walking in the right direction. "Getting in everyone's way, tripping us up or almost knocking us over. *And* he kept pulling things out of boxes and running off with them."

"He probably thought he was helping," Mandy chuckled.

"That's what *I* said," James told her. "But Mum and Dad didn't agree."

"Poor Blackie," Mandy said, bending to stroke him. Blackie sat down suddenly and James almost fell over him.

"Whoops!" Mandy laughed. "Sorry, James. That was my fault."

They straightened themselves out and started walking again.

"Here you are," said Mr Hunter as they reached the car. "You've been so long I thought you'd taken Blackie home, Mandy. I imagined you'd decided to keep him with you while *we* went on holiday," he joked. The Hunters were having a long weekend in the Lake District.

"I wish I could," Mandy replied. "I'm really going to miss him." She bent to give the Labrador a final pat. Then James put him in the back of the car, behind the special dog guard.

"*I'm* going to miss Benji," James said. "Look, he's sitting on the wall, watching. I'm sure he's upset about being left behind."

"James! If you don't get in, we'll leave *you* behind as well," said Mrs Hunter, popping her head out of the car window. "Stop worrying about Benji. He'll be fine with Mrs Padgett looking after him."

Mrs Padgett was the Hunters' next-door neighbour. She loved cats and Benji was very fond of her.

"Yes, I suppose you're right," James said as he scrambled into the car. "OK, Dad. I'm ready!"

"Bye, James!" Mandy called as the car set off. "Have a great time. I'll see you in three days!"

Mandy waved until the car turned the corner. Then she turned to look at Benji. She was just in time to see his tail disappearing round the side of Mrs Padgett's house. So Benji didn't seem to mind about being left behind, after all!

Mandy smiled and set off for home. She lived at the other end of the village from James in an old stone cottage called Animal Ark. It was a good name. Mr and Mrs Hope, Mandy's parents, were vets and their surgery was attached to the house.

There was only one car parked outside Animal Ark when Mandy got there, which meant morning surgery was nearly over. Mandy recognised the car. It was Mrs Todd's.

Mrs Todd was Mandy's teacher. She had a spaniel called Jodie. Mandy was just wondering what was wrong with Jodie when Mrs Todd came out of the surgery door. Jodie was prancing happily at her side. Mandy smiled; there didn't seem to be much wrong with her at all.

"Hello, Mandy," said Mrs Todd. "Jodie's just had her booster injection."

"Hello, Mrs Todd," Mandy replied as she bent down to stroke the spaniel. "I was a bit worried when I saw your car

here. I'm glad there isn't anything wrong with her."

Mandy petted the lively dog for a few seconds. Then she looked up at her teacher. "Are you enjoying your holiday, Mrs Todd?" she asked.

"Yes, thank you. I am," Mrs Todd replied. "But there isn't much left of it now. Just over a week to go."

"I know." Mandy nodded her head.

"Mum's taking me into Walton to get some new school shoes this afternoon."

"No James today, then?" Mrs Todd wasn't James's teacher. James was eight, a year younger than Mandy and in a different class. But Mrs Todd knew they were best friends.

"He's gone away for three days with his mum and dad," Mandy said, looking sad. "They'll be staying in a caravan so they've taken Blackie with them. I'm starting to miss them already and I've only just seen them off!"

"Never mind, Mandy," said Mrs Todd with a kind smile. "Three days isn't long. They'll be back before you know it."

"I suppose so," Mandy replied. "I bet Blackie will get up to all sorts of mischief in the caravan. And on the beach," she added. "James will have loads to tell me when he gets back."

"I expect you'll have a lot to tell James as well, Mandy. Just you wait and see," said Mrs Todd.

Mandy smiled. Mrs Todd was right. Three days wasn't long. Not really. She'd have to find plenty of things to do to stop her from missing James and Blackie too much.

2

A new friend

"Hi, Jean," Mandy said, standing on tiptoe to peer over the reception desk. "Wow! What happened?"

Jean Knox, Animal Ark's receptionist, was kneeling on the floor surrounded by a sea of paper, envelopes and postcards.

"Hi, Mandy!" Jean glanced up. "Mrs

Todd's Jodie happened, that's what! She jumped up at the desk to say hello to me and managed to knock everything off."

"Sounds like the sort of thing Blackie would do," Mandy said. She went round to help Jean sort out the mess.

"You can put these postcards into their envelopes if you like," Jean said. "They're reminders, to let people know that their pets are due for a booster injection. They were all in order until Jodie knocked them down. You'll have to sort them out carefully, though. Make sure you put the correct card in each envelope."

"Or Mrs Stafford might wonder why she's been asked to bring Rover to Animal Ark when she's got a cat called Pixie!" Mandy chuckled.

"I see you're back from seeing James off, Mandy!" Mrs Hope's head appeared over the desk. "But what *are* you two doing down there?" she added.

"Hi, Mum," Mandy said. "Jodie knocked everything on to the floor. I'm

helping Jean to put the reminder cards into their envelopes."

"That's good," Mrs Hope said. "I've just got one or two house calls to make before lunch. Dad should be back at about two o'clock. We'll go and get your new shoes then, Mandy."

"Where is Dad?" Mandy asked.

Mrs Hope smiled. "He's up at Giants Farm doing some blood tests on Mr Grove's cows."

Mandy giggled. It always made her laugh when she thought of Mr Grove living at Giants Farm. He was such a small man! His farm was called Giants Farm because it was near a huge rock called the Giant's Seat.

"Oh, Mandy, Gran phoned to see if you wanted to go round for tea," Mrs Hope added. "I said we'd call in at Lilac Cottage on our way back from Walton."

"Great!" said Mandy. "I can't wait to find out if the new people have moved in yet!"

"Well, you haven't got long to wait now," Jean said with a smile. She handed Mandy a few envelopes. "There, I think that's all of them."

"Yup!" Mandy checked the floor, then dragged a chair over to Jean's small desk and set to work.

"I hope it rains soon," Mandy said to her mum. They were on their way back from Walton. And, as well as her school shoes,

Mandy also had a new pair of wellies. She couldn't wait to wear them.

Mrs Hope laughed. "Don't let the farmers hear you wishing for rain, Mandy. Not until they've got their harvest in!"

"Grandad would like it to rain," Mandy said. "He told me that the hot, dry weather makes gardening hard work. Oh, look," she added, "there's a car outside Jasmine Cottage. The new people must have moved in. Drive a bit slower, Mum. I want to see if I can see anyone."

Mandy twisted in her seat to get a better look. "Nope," she said. "But they *have* moved in. There's curtains up in the windows."

"I expect Gran will be able to tell you all about them," said Mrs Hope as she pulled up outside Lilac Cottage. "She's sure to have welcomed them to Welford."

"Gran met them when they came to look at the cottage," said Mandy. "She said there's a boy a bit younger than me. I don't know if he's got any pets, though."

"I'm sure you'll find that out soon enough!" Mrs Hope chuckled, then added, "Here's Gran now."

Mandy jumped out of the car and ran up the garden path. "Hi, Gran. Just wait until you see my new wellies!"

"Hello, Mandy, love. I wasn't expecting you so soon. I was just going to take these tomatoes round to Mrs Jackson."

Grandad popped his head out of the greenhouse door, chuckling. "I expect you could persuade Mandy to take them for you, Dorothy."

Mandy laughed. She ran over to give Grandad a hug. "You bet I will!" she said.

Mrs Jackson lived two doors away from Lilac Cottage. Her cottage was called Rose Cottage. Every summer the grey stonework was almost hidden by the roses that climbed up every wall and around the doors and windows.

Mrs Jackson's daughter, Jane, had a pony called Prince. Mandy loved all animals but Jane's pony was one of her special favourites. She nearly always went to see him when she visited her grandparents.

"And I bet you'd like a nice carrot for Prince," Grandad said. "I've just dug some up for your mum to take home. Come and choose one; then we'll give it a rinse under the garden tap."

A few minutes later Mandy went off with the bag of tomatoes and a juicy carrot. An unfamiliar boy was running along ahead of her. She wondered if he was the new boy from Jasmine Cottage.

Suddenly, he tripped up and fell to the ground with a thump.

Mandy gasped and ran to catch up with him. "Are you OK?" she asked, kneeling down beside him. "Have you hurt yourself?"

"I banged my knee really hard!" he said. He rolled over into a sitting position

and peered at it. "I think I landed on a stone or something," he added. "It's just scraped. I'll be OK when it stops stinging."

"Where were you going in such a hurry?" Mandy asked.

The boy looked up and smiled. "There's a fantastic pony in the orchard here. I was on my way to see if he'd make friends with me."

"He's called Prince," Mandy told him. "He is a lovely pony and I'm sure he'll make friends. But I think you should get your knee seen to first. Look, it's bleeding, and you've got some dirt in it."

"Is that you, Mandy?" a voice called from behind the thick, high hedge.

"Yes it is, Mrs Jackson," Mandy called back. "And . . . what's your name?" she asked the boy.

"I'm Paul Stevens," he told her. "We've just moved in to Jasmine Cottage."

"And Paul from Jasmine Cottage is here, too, Mrs Jackson. He's hurt his knee."

"Well, you'd better bring him in, Mandy. I'll meet you at the gate."

Mandy picked up the bag of tomatoes. Then she and Paul walked to Mrs Jackson's gate. Mrs Jackson looked down at Paul's knee. "It doesn't look too bad," she said. "Come on, we'll go indoors and ask Jane to bathe it for you."

"I was running to look at the pony," Paul said as they went up the garden path. "I love ponies. And dogs and cats and things as well."

"You and Mandy will find plenty to talk about, then," Mrs Jackson said. She opened the back door and called out for Jane.

"Jane's fifteen. She's going in for nursing when she leaves school," Mrs Jackson told Paul as Jane got the first-aid box down. "She loves opportunities like this. She's always wanted to be a nurse."

"Just like I've always wanted a pony," Paul said. "And now we've come to live in Welford, I'm getting one! That's why I was coming to see *your* pony. I wanted to tell him all about it. I couldn't tell anyone else 'cos I don't know anyone here yet."

"Well, you know us now," Mandy said. "You can tell us all about it."

3

Exciting plans

"There," Mrs Jackson said proudly. "Jane's made a nice neat job of your knee, Paul. Does it feel better now?"

Paul ran his fingers over the strip of plaster Jane had put on the graze. "Yes, thank you, it does!" He nodded and slid off the high stool Jane had sat him on.

"How about a nice drink of rosehip cordial?" Mrs Jackson asked.

"Um . . ." Paul looked across at Mandy.

Mandy laughed. "I think Paul's longing to see Prince," she told Mrs Jackson. "And I'm dying to hear about the pony he's getting! Maybe we could have something to drink afterwards?"

"We'll put the drinks on a tray and take them to the orchard with us," Mrs Jackson said, her eyes twinkling merrily. "*I* want to hear all about Paul's pony, too!"

"Brilliant!" Paul said and dashed to the door. "Come on, Mandy!"

"Go on, you two," Mrs Jackson told them. "I'll catch you up with the drinks."

Paul certainly seems to like ponies, Mandy thought as they dashed along to the orchard. She felt sure she was going to like him – and that James would too!

Mandy loved the smell of the different fruits when the sun was shining down on them. The trees grew at either side of the orchard behind fences made of rosewood. Prince couldn't reach the apples, pears and plums that weighed the branches down – he grazed happily and safely in the rest of the orchard.

Jane gave a whistle and the little Welsh pony trotted eagerly towards them.

"I won't be able to do that with my pony," Paul sighed, holding his hand out for Prince to smell it.

"Oh, you will, Paul," Jane told him. "It doesn't take long for a pony to recognise a whistle."

Paul rubbed Prince's soft nose and looked glum. "But I *can't* whistle!" he blurted out.

"No problem," Mandy said. "My friend James is excellent at whistling. I'm sure he'll teach you when he comes home, Paul!"

Paul cheered up immediately. Mandy broke her carrot in two and handed him a piece. "Here," she said. "Give it to Prince. He loves carrots."

Prince's velvety nose twitched as Paul held the carrot out. His top lip moved as though he were smiling, then he moved his mouth closer to Paul's hand. Paul chuckled as Prince gently took the carrot.

"He tickled my fingers!" Paul said in delight. "I *knew* he was a fantastic pony the minute I saw him! Oh, I hope mine will be as nice!"

Mrs Jackson arrived just then, carrying a tray with four tall glasses of bright-pink rosehip cordial.

"Right, Paul. Tell us about this pony before you burst!" she said as she handed out the glasses.

"Well," Paul said, his eyes shining brightly, "someone came round from the Horse and Pony Rescue Sanctuary in Glisterdale this morning to look at our paddock and stable. They wanted to talk to us to make sure we were the right sort of people to give one of their ponies a home!" He stopped to catch his breath. But Mandy couldn't wait to hear the rest.

"And?" she said excitedly. "What did they say?"

"They said yes!" Paul grinned happily. "And . . . we're going to the sanctuary tomorrow to choose one!"

Prince nuzzled Paul's ear and whinnied softly. Everyone laughed.

"Prince thinks it's terrific news!" Jane said.

"It is, isn't it!" said Paul, stroking Prince's silky neck. "I can hardly wait for tomorrow!"

"You ought to ask Mandy to go with you, Paul," said Jane. "Her mum and dad are the local vets, so she knows quite a bit about animals."

Mandy smiled. She wasn't allowed to help with the sick animals who came to Animal Ark, but her mum and dad told her all about their illnesses and what they were going to do to make them better. And Mandy had read every single one of the pamphlets in the waiting room on caring for animals.

"Would you, Mandy?" said Paul. "Would you come with us?"

"Wow! *Would* I!" Mandy laughed. "But I'd better check it out with my parents first. My mum's at Gran and Grandad's — they live just up the road at Lilac Cottage."

"Let's go and ask now!" said Paul. He finished his drink in one gulp then wiped his hand across his mouth. "That was delicious, Mrs Jackson. Thank you."

"Yes!" Mandy agreed. "Thanks."

"Off you go then," Mrs Jackson said. "And thank your gran and grandad for the tomatoes, won't you, Mandy?"

"I will!" Mandy said. "Bye, Prince. We'll come and see you again soon."

"Yes, we promise," said Paul. Then he and Mandy hurried off.

"As soon as you get your pony and it's settled in, Paul, let me know. Then I can come round to see it!" Jane called out after them.

"Look, Mandy!" Paul said when they reached Lilac Cottage. "That's my mum in the garden with your gran and grandad! Is the lady with red hair your mum?"

"Yup!" Mandy nodded. "It seems our mums have already got to know each other!" The children dashed up the garden path.

"I see you and Paul have already met, Mandy!" her mum said. "Hello, Paul. I'm Mrs Hope."

"Hello," Paul replied breathlessly. "Mum, this is Mandy. And . . . and . . .

please can she come with us tomorrow to help choose my pony?"

The grown-ups looked at one another and laughed.

"What's the matter?" Mandy and Paul said together.

"Paul's mum has just been asking if Dad or I would go to the sanctuary with them to check over the pony they choose," Mrs Hope explained to Mandy. "We'd already fixed for you to come, too!"

4

The sad pony

Next morning, the Stevenses came to pick Mandy up straight after breakfast. She'd agreed to travel with them; Mrs Hope was going in her own car in case she got any emergency calls.

Mandy got in the back of the car with Paul. "Hi, Mandy," he said excitedly.

"We've got to keep an eye on the horse box for Dad. He isn't used to towing one. It isn't ours; we hired it when the sanctuary people said we'd be able to bring our pony home right away! Gosh, I can't wait to get there!"

"Paul!" Mrs Stevens laughed. "You're like a runaway train!"

Mandy laughed too. "But it's so exciting, Mrs Stevens. I can't wait either."

It wasn't a very long journey to Glisterdale, but to Mandy and Paul the ride seemed endless. At last they saw the sign for the Horse and Pony Rescue Sanctuary and Mr Stevens turned off the main road.

"These fields must belong to the sanctuary," said Mandy. "Look, there's loads of ponies grazing and wandering around and . . . Oh, look, Paul! There's a big cart-horse and some donkeys, too!"

Mrs Stevens twisted in her seat. "We're not having a donkey or a cart-horse,

Paul," she said teasingly. "Only a pony."

"I know, Mum." Paul chuckled. "Only a pony! But I do like donkeys," he added.

"Well, here we are," Mr Stevens said.

Paul gulped as the car drew to a stop. "I feel all funny inside, now we're really here," he said.

Mandy laughed. "You'll soon feel OK when you start looking properly at the ponies," she told him.

The sanctuary manager came out of a nearby stable block to greet them. "That's where we keep the newest arrivals," she told them. "There's a large run-out area at the back of the stables so they can go outside whenever they like. We keep them separate from all the others for a few weeks to give them a chance to settle in."

"And in case they've got something the others can catch?" Mandy asked.

The manager nodded. "There speaks the daughter of a vet," she said, smiling at Mrs Hope.

"Well we won't look at the ones in the stable block, then," said Paul. "It would be *ages* before I could have one of them!"

The manager smiled again. "Come on," she said, "I'll take you to the paddock where we keep the ponies who *are* ready to go to a new home. It's only just down here."

They followed the manager along a wide gravelled path with fields either side. Mandy saw some foals playing together. She'd have liked to have a closer look but she knew Paul wouldn't want to stop.

But suddenly, he *did* stop. He was staring at a brownish-grey pony in one of the fenced-off fields. The pony was a few metres away from the fence and was looking straight at Paul.

Mandy's heart lurched. The pony had such sad, sad eyes that peered out from under a dull, heavy fringe of dark-brown hair. One eye looked smaller than the other and Mandy realised it was a bit swollen and puffy underneath. His coat was dull too, and his ribs stuck out. He was really thin and Mandy caught her breath when she saw a few nasty-looking sores, and the scars and patches that covered the pony's back and sides.

The pony started moving very slowly towards the fence. His eyes seemed to be fixed on Paul. Mandy heard Paul take a deep, wobbly breath. Then he crept delicately up to the fence.

Paul and the pony arrived at the fence at exactly the same moment. For a split second they just stared at each other. Then the pony whinnied softly and laid his big broad head on Paul's shoulder.

"My word!" said the sanctuary manager. "That's the first noise Paddy's made since he came here. And it's the first time he's *ever* wanted to make friends with anyone! He's such a sad pony!"

Paul held his hand out for Paddy to sniff. Then, carefully and gently, he stroked the pony's greyish muzzle. Paddy

breathed heavily and made a soft whickering noise. When Paul stopped stroking him, the pony pushed his face into Paul's neck.

"He's asking you to stroke him again," whispered Mandy, coming to stand close to Paul.

"I don't have to choose a pony!" Paul said. "Paddy's chosen *me*!"

But the sanctuary manager shook her head. "I think Paddy will have to be one of our permanent residents," she said. "We rescued him a few months ago from someone who'd treated him very badly indeed."

She walked quietly forward and pointed to the scars on Paddy's back. "These are from where he'd been whipped," she explained. "He was covered in nasty sores, he was starving and his left eye was bruised and swollen. His eye isn't quite right yet and we bathe it twice a day for him. The scars will fade a little bit more in time but we still have to put special ointment on some of them. They were worse than all the others and are taking longer to heal."

"But I could do all that if you showed me what to do," said Paul. "Mandy would help me, wouldn't you, Mandy?"

Mandy nodded. "And I'm sure James would as well," she said.

"Paul, I really think you should look at some of the other ponies," Mrs Stevens said. "I'm sure you'll see one you like."

"I won't see one I like as much as Paddy!" said Paul. "Paddy's special. He chose me and . . . and look! He *trusts* me."

Paddy's head was resting on Paul's shoulder again. The scarred pony's eyes were half-closed and his body was swaying gently. Mrs Stevens moved over to them and stood behind Paul to look at Paddy. The pony blew softly into her face.

"See, Mum. Paddy likes you, too," Paul said.

"What do you think now you've seen them together?" Mrs Stevens asked the manager.

"Paddy does seem to have taken to your son," the manager replied thoughtfully. "And he blew at you. That's a sign of friendship. He certainly didn't want to be friends with any of us. I think maybe we *shouldn't* dismiss it out of hand. Paul's right. The pony does seem to trust him. That would help enormously in getting Paddy *properly* better. But Paul would have a lot of hard work in front of him."

Paul looked pleadingly at his mum and dad.

"Let's ask Mrs Hope to examine Paddy and see what she says," suggested Mr Stevens. His wife nodded.

Mrs Hope had a few quiet words with the sanctuary manager and Paul's parents. Mandy and Paul stood by Paddy, petting him and talking to him. Then the manager hurried away towards one of the buildings.

"Right, Paul," Mrs Hope said. "The manager has gone for a bridle and leading rein. We're going to see if Paddy will let you lead him around the field. If he does, I want to watch carefully to see how he moves and behaves. Then, if everything there seems OK, I'll give him a good checking-over."

The manager came back and fixed on the leading rein. "All right, Paul. Come into the field now," she said quietly.

"Don't go behind Paddy," Mandy whispered. "Let him see you walking towards him, Paul."

"I know you shouldn't walk up behind ponies," said Paul. "I had some riding lessons where we used to live."

"Go on, then!" Mandy smiled. "And good luck." She wished she could go into the field and walk with Paddy and Paul. But Mandy knew that it was something Paul had to do by himself. She moved over to stand next to her mum, crossed her fingers and watched anxiously.

Paddy behaved really well. He seemed to enjoy walking along beside Paul. Paul led him right to the other end of the field.

A road ran past the end of the field and Mandy held her breath when a very noisy motorbike whizzed by, close to the hedge. But Paddy stayed calm and quiet.

"He heard it, though," Mrs Hope murmured. "I saw his ears pricking forward. I think he could be an Exmoor pony. They can be nervous."

"Oh, I don't want Paul to have a nervous pony," said Mrs Stevens, looking worried.

"No, no, I don't think Paddy is," Mrs Hope told her. "We'll see how he behaves when I examine him."

"You mean you think Paddy's OK so far, Mum?" Mandy asked.

Mrs Hope smiled. "Maybe. But let's wait and see."

When Paul brought Paddy back up to Mrs Hope, she told him to come out of the field. "You can watch from this side of the fence while I examine him," she added with a smile.

"OK," Paul replied. "But how long will it take?" He looked very anxious.

"Not too long, but I expect it will seem like a long time to you."

Paul and Mandy watched as Mrs Hope looked in Paddy's eyes and his mouth. She listened to his heart and chest, and ran gentle fingers over his body and down his legs.

Mandy held her breath when her mum picked up one of Paddy's feet. She knew ponies often didn't like that. Paul seemed to know, too, because he was holding on tight to the fence post.

But Paddy didn't seem to mind. When Mrs Hope picked up one of his back feet, he even turned his head to nibble gently at the top of her hair.

At last, Mrs Hope finished. She patted Paddy and climbed nimbly over the fence. "Well," she said, "considering what Paddy's been through, he's really quite healthy. His coat should improve with a lot of hard work and attention, and his scars will fade eventually."

Mandy nudged Paul and showed him her crossed fingers. Paul nodded. His fingers were crossed, too.

"He *is* an Exmoor pony," Mrs Hope added. "He's got seven molar teeth. Only Exmoors have seven."

"You said Exmoors could be nervous," said Mr Stevens.

"Mmm." Mrs Hope nodded thoughtfully. "The breed takes its name from the high, wild moorland in the south-west of the country. There are still more or less untamed herds running on Exmoor and they don't have much contact with humans. But some of the ponies are taken off the moor for breeding. And some settle down well enough in a new environment and come to trust people. I think Paddy is one of those."

Mrs Hope reached out and rubbed Paddy's muzzle. Then she turned to the manager. "I'd like to blanket-saddle him and see if he'll let Paul mount him. Whoever rode him before obviously gave him a bad time. He might not like the idea of being ridden again."

The manager went off to fetch a thick blanket and a lightweight saddle. Mandy and Paul leaned on the fence and stroked Paddy again.

"It'll be OK, Paddy," Paul said quietly. "Where I used to go riding, they said I was very good at getting on to ponies' backs. And I'll be ever so gentle with you, I promise I will."

"You won't actually be able to ride Paddy yet, Paul," Mrs Hope told him. "It'll be a little while before he can be ridden. Those last few sores need to be completely cleared up first. But we'll see if Paddy will let you sit on him for a few minutes and maybe take a few steps. If he does, as long as you understand he'll need a lot of care and attention . . . well, I think maybe he could be a good pony for you."

★

"Oh, Mum, look at Paul's face! I wish we had a camera with us," said Mandy.

Paul was grinning so widely the corners of his lips nearly reached the straps of the riding hat the manager had insisted that he wore. He was sitting on a small saddle that had been placed over a soft, thick blanket on Paddy's back. And Paddy seemed more than happy for Paul to be there.

"OK, Paul," said the sanctuary manager, "I'll hold the leading rein and we'll just see if Paddy is willing to walk. Only a few paces, though," she added.

Paul clicked his tongue and whispered, "Walk on, Paddy!"

The pony didn't hesitate. And when Paul said "Whoa, boy," Paddy came to a gentle stop.

Smiling, the sanctuary manager lifted Paul down. They were both careful not to touch Paddy's sore parts.

"Well done, Paul," said Mandy. "And well done, Paddy!"

Paul went round to Paddy's head and put his arms around the pony's neck. "They can't say no now!" he whispered. "You'll be coming home with me, Paddy. And soon you'll have lots of new friends. I know you're going to love everything."

"We wouldn't usually let a pony leave here while it still needed treatment," the sanctuary manager told Paul. "But I've talked it over with your mum and dad, and Mrs Hope says she'll show you exactly how to bathe Paddy's eyes and put the drops in, and how to put the special ointment on his sores. And she or Mr Hope will check Paddy over every few days."

"You can come and visit him any time you like," said Paul. "He'll have the best home a pony's ever had! Can we get him into the horse box now?"

At first, Paddy didn't want to go into the horse box. But when Paul ran up the ramp and called the pony, Paddy decided that he'd go in after all.

While Paul's parents were checking the box was firmly shut and locked, Mrs Hope looked down at Mandy. "I know you'd love to go back with them," she said. "But I think Paul should settle Paddy in on his own."

"OK, Mum," Mandy agreed. "I suppose you're right. Will it be OK if I say I'll call round to Jasmine Cottage tomorrow?"

"Yes. If it's all right with Paul's mum and dad, it's all right with me." Mrs Hope smiled and ruffled Mandy's hair.

5

The best of friends

When they got back to Animal Ark, Jean told Mandy that James had phoned. "Mrs Hunter's got a really bad cold so they're going to come home a day early," she explained. "They'll be home late tonight and James said to tell you he'll be round in the morning."

"Poor Mrs Hunter," said Mandy. "But it's great that James will be here tomorrow. I'll make a 'welcome home' card and go and put it through his letterbox. I don't want anyone to tell him about Paul and Paddy so I'll write an extra message on it. I'm going to tell him to come round as soon as he can in the morning and not to talk to anyone first!"

"Poor James." Mrs Hope laughed. "He'll be longing to find out what's going on when he reads that!"

James arrived at Animal Ark at half past eight. He was holding his welcome home card and he still looked half asleep. His brown hair was ruffled and the lace on one of his trainers hadn't been fastened.

"Welcome home, James!" Mandy said at once. "So much has happened while you were away!"

James asked what her mysterious message meant.

"I have a surprise for you," Mandy

replied. "But it's not here," she added, with a mischievous grin. "We'll have to go somewhere first."

It didn't take them long to cycle to Jasmine Cottage. Paul was waiting for them at the gate. "I've just phoned Animal Ark," he said. "Your dad told me you were on your way, Mandy. He's coming round to see Paddy later. Is this James?"

"Yes it is." Mandy quickly introduced the two boys. "James came home a day early, Paul. I knew you wouldn't mind him coming round with me."

"Have you told him about Paddy? Have you asked him about teaching me to whistle?" asked Paul.

"Mandy hasn't told me anything yet," said James, more confused than he already was. "Only that she's got a surprise for me," he continued. "But you mentioned me teaching you to whistle. So . . . I guess the surprise is a dog. A dog called Paddy!"

Paul grinned. "Come on, let's go and see him. He's in the paddock."

"Oh!" said James when they reached the paddock. "Paddy's a *pony*! He's . . . he's . . ." James glanced at Mandy and she knew her friend was disturbed at the pony's ragged appearance.

"Paul got Paddy from the Horse and Pony Rescue Sanctuary," Mandy said, explaining everything to James.

"He's going to need a lot of looking after to get him really well again," Paul added. "And Mandy said you'd both help me."

"Of course we will," said James shoving his glasses further on to his nose.

"Can you get Paddy to come to us, Paul?" asked Mandy. "We can introduce him to James, then."

"I'm not sure," Paul replied. "We tried to put him in his stable last night, but he didn't want to go in. So we let him stay out in the paddock. When I called him this morning he wouldn't come to me. I think he thought I was going to take him to the stable again.

"He lets *me* go to *him*," Paul continued, "and doesn't run off. But he doesn't seem to want to move from the middle of the paddock. I really want to see if Paddy will let me groom him."

"The paddock's a good place to do that," said Mandy. "Let's go and get his brushes!"

Paddy whinnied loudly as the three of them made their way across the paddock. "And he's swishing his tail!" said Mandy. "That's a good sign. I think he's pleased to see us."

Paddy *was* pleased to see them. He lay his big broad head on each shoulder in turn and even tried to lick James's glasses!

After they'd petted and stroked Paddy for a while, Paul ran a dandy-brush gently over the pony's body. "You're supposed to use a circular movement with this brush really," he said. "Then the stiff bristles remove any dirt. But I just want

him to get used to the feel of the different brushes first."

"Good idea," said Mandy, nodding. She picked up another brush and started to brush Paddy's mane. Then, while Paul brushed the pony's tail, James ran a soft brush over Paddy's ribs.

"Poor Paddy," said James. "He's very thin, isn't he? Look at his sticky-out ribs! And his coat needs some work."

"We'll soon have him looking right," said Mandy, kissing Paddy's muzzle, then laughing as Paddy blew hard down his nostrils.

Mr Hope said exactly the same thing when he came to check Paddy over. "Lots of loving, plenty of grooming, careful attention to his eye and his sores, a small helping of barley and linseed mash for his breakfast every day, halibut liver oil and malt at midday, plus his usual feed. All that, and you'll soon have him looking right."

"He won't go into his stable, Mr Hope," said Paul. "Will he be OK if we leave him out at night?"

"Yes, he'll be fine, Paul. And by the time it's winter, Paddy will be really used to you and his new home. By then, he'll probably look forward to going in his stable at night."

The next few days passed quickly. Mandy and James spent most of the time with

Paul and Paddy. James managed to teach Paul to whistle, and Paddy began to trot up to Paul whenever he heard the sound! Paul couldn't whistle at Paddy when Blackie was there, though, because the gangly-legged Labrador kept jumping up at him and making him laugh!

Mandy had been a bit worried the first time James brought Blackie with him. She'd read in one of her parents' animal care books that Exmoors were sometimes nervous of dogs. But Paddy and Blackie rubbed noses and were the best of friends right from the start!

Jane Jackson brought Paul a large white silk scarf. "If you put it over Paddy's soft grooming brush every time you use it, his coat will soon start to shine," she told Paul.

Paddy was looking better every day. He was still underweight and his scars hadn't faded much more, but his eye wasn't so swollen and his sores were almost completely healed.

One morning, Paul decided to surprise Mandy and James. He put Paddy on a leading rein and walked him down to the end of the lane to meet them. "It will get him used to the area for when I can ride him," he told them.

"And to the sound of traffic from the road into the village," Mandy added, rubbing her cheek over Paddy's soft muzzle.

"Paddy really likes walking along the lane," James said. "See how he's looking around, as if he's saying 'hello' to every tree and bush."

"And to every clump of grass." Paul laughed as the pony lowered his head and started to graze. "But I don't really like him eating this grass. Too many traffic fumes on it."

"I've brought him a carrot," said James. "That will distract him." He offered Paddy the carrot and Blackie woofed indignantly. "OK, OK." James laughed. "I've got a treat for you, as well."

The three friends spent the whole morning grooming Paddy in the paddock. Mandy's gran popped in to see them and invited them to lunch. "Not you, Paddy," she said. "You can have yours here. I've brought you some more carrots and a nice sweet apple."

They all had things to do after lunch. Mandy was going to the dentist, Mrs Hunter was taking James to visit relations and Paul's mum was taking him into Walton to have his hair cut ready for starting school. But Mrs Stevens said there was just time for Paul to walk Paddy to the end of the lane to see Mandy and James off.

"I can't believe we go back to school tomorrow," said Mandy as they walked along. "The time's gone really quickly since you got Paddy, Paul."

"I'm looking forward to coming to your school," Paul replied. "But I hope people are friendly."

"Oh, they will be, Paul. Wait and see

– you'll soon have loads of friends."

They were almost at the end of the lane when Paddy lowered his head and tried to nibble at the grass on the verge again.

"No, Paddy!" Paul said sternly. "You are *not* to do that!"

Mandy and James watched as Paul tried to make Paddy lift his head. "You're a naughty pony!" Paul said. He *sounded* cross, but Mandy and James could tell he was trying not to laugh. At last, Paul managed to persuade Paddy to stop nibbling.

Further up the lane on the other side, Mandy saw a lady and a girl standing still and staring hard at them.

Mandy recognised the girl. It was Tina Cunningham. She was in James's class at school. She was just about to wave when Tina and her mum turned and carried on up the lane.

Mandy didn't think any more about it. She and James said goodbye to Paul and Paddy, then hurried off.

"Why does today feel different?" Mandy murmured when she woke up the next morning. Then she realised why: the summer holidays were over. She was going back to school!

"It'll be great to see my school-friends again and talk about what we've all done in the holidays," Mandy said over breakfast.

"Don't get talking so much that you forget about Paul," Mrs Hope reminded her with a smile.

"Don't worry, Mum," Mandy replied. "James and I aren't cycling to school today. We're meeting Paul at the end of his lane, so when we get to school we'll introduce him to all our friends and help him settle in. James is going to ask Mrs Black if he can take Paul round school to show him where everything is."

Mandy ran to get her coat and backpack. Then she said goodbye and dashed off to meet James and Paul.

Paul was a few minutes late. "I had to explain to Paddy why I wouldn't be seeing much of him today," he said. "I really didn't want to say goodbye."

"There's still plenty of time," Mandy said. "There just won't be as *much* time to talk to everybody before the bell goes."

When the three of them walked into the playground, Mandy saw her friend Carrie. "Come on," said Mandy. "Here's someone I think you'll like."

But Carrie didn't seem very friendly, and she didn't even *look* at Paul when Mandy tried to introduce him!

Then Sarah Drummond walked past without speaking. She was in Mandy's class but she usually talked quite a lot to James. Sarah's Labrador, Sooty, was from the same litter as Blackie. Normally she would ask James how Sooty's brother was getting on.

When Mandy saw Jill Redfern and asked how Toto, her tortoise, was, Jill mumbled something and then hurried away. And three of the juniors – Susan Davis, Laura Baker and Jack Gardiner – who usually loved chatting to Mandy and James, ran off when they saw Mandy, James and Paul walking towards them.

Mandy couldn't understand it. It couldn't be because Paul was a new boy! Usually, everyone at Welford Primary School thought it was great when someone new started there. They would at least come over and say hello!

Just then Amy Fenton arrived. "Gosh!" she said, dashing up to Mandy. "I made it before the bell. I thought I was going to be really late. Minnie got out of her cage and it took me ages to catch her and put her back in."

Mandy laughed. Maybe she was just imagining that the others had been acting strangely. Amy was certainly friendly enough. "Minnie is Amy's mouse," she told Paul.

"And this is Paul Stevens," James told

Amy. "He's come to live in Jasmine Cottage near Mandy's grandparents."

"Hi, Paul!" Amy smiled. "Have *you* got any pets?"

The bell went before Paul could reply, and everyone made a mad dash to line up ready for going inside. James took Paul with him and stood behind him.

James was surprised to feel someone poking him hard in the back and to hear a fierce whisper: "You and Mandy Hope should be ashamed of yourselves!"

He swung round to see Tina Cunningham glaring scornfully at him. There was no time to ask Tina what she meant; the second bell rang and they all went inside and into their classrooms.

6

A terrible mistake

When Mandy got to her classroom, she began to feel uneasy again. Nobody called out to her to go and sit next to them. Nobody asked her what she'd done in the holidays or told her what they'd done. And when she walked over to look at Terry and Jerry, the class gerbils, she was almost sure she heard someone say that Terry and Jerry had better watch out!

Mandy was really glad when it was time to go into assembly. Then she'd be able to sit next to James and try to figure out why everyone was being so unfriendly.

But James didn't seem to want to talk, either. When Mandy hurried over to sit next to him, he stared straight ahead with a really serious look on his face. Mandy leaned forward to look at Paul, who was sitting next to James. Paul's shoulders were hunched and he was staring down at his feet. Had she done something wrong?

Amy Fenton was on Mandy's other side. Mandy turned her head to say something to her. But Amy whispered, "I wish I'd never spoken to you, Mandy. I'm so surprised!" Amy stopped whispering as Mrs Garvie, the Headteacher, stepped on to the platform.

Mandy usually enjoyed Mrs Garvie's start of term talks. But today she didn't hear a single word! She was too busy wondering what on earth was going on.

At break, Mandy tried to find James. Maybe he had some explanation for why everyone was ignoring her. But she couldn't see him anywhere. Paul was in the playground, though, and he walked slowly towards her.

"I hate your school, Mandy. You told me it was the best ever! But it isn't. Nobody wants to be friends with me. They won't even *talk* to me. I wish we'd never come to live in Welford. I hate it here!"

Before Mandy could say anything to try and comfort Paul, he dashed away and disappeared into the boys' washroom. Wasn't there anyone who would talk to her?

At lunch-time, James came up to Mandy. "I needed to see you without Paul being here," he said quickly. "I don't know what's going on, Mandy, but whatever it

is I'm sure it's something to do with Paul!"

Mandy nodded. "Maybe you're right, James. We've got to find out what it is and try to make things OK."

"We sure have!" James nodded fiercely and his glasses slid down his nose. "But I don't know how! Except . . ." he added thoughtfully. He told Mandy what Tina Cunningham had said to him earlier on. "But I've no idea what she was talking about!"

"So we go and ask her what she meant,"

Mandy said determinedly. "Look, there she is, over there with some of the others."

Mandy went straight over to where Tina and her friends were standing. But she didn't even get a chance to confront Tina.

"You and James should be ashamed of yourselves, Mandy Hope!" Tina began, as soon as Mandy was within earshot. "None of us can understand how you can talk to someone who's so cruel to his pony! I saw how badly that pony's being treated!"

Just at that moment, Paul came up. Tina pointed at him and continued loudly. "And I saw how *that* boy wouldn't let the pony eat the grass when the poor thing is so thin you can see its bones sticking out! He shouldn't be allowed to keep a pony. I told them all about it at the stables when I went for my riding lesson. They said I should report it to someone!"

Paul took a couple of steps towards

Tina. "You've got it wrong!" he said. "Paddy is—"

"Paddy?" scoffed Tina. "More like *Patchy*, if you ask me. That pony is a mess!"

Paul made a strange gasping noise. Then, sobbing loudly, he ran off. He was running so quickly Mandy didn't think she'd be able to catch up with him. She was probably too cross to have tried to stop him anyway.

She marched up to Tina and stood squarely in front of her. "Now just you listen to me, Tina Cunningham!" Mandy's voice trembled with anger as she continued. "Paul's pony came from the rescue sanctuary. He'd been so badly treated by his previous owner that the sanctuary manager thought he'd have to stay there forever. Paddy didn't want to be friends with anyone until he saw Paul! And Paul really had to persuade everyone to let him have Paddy! I know how hard *that* was, because I was there . . . and so was my mum!"

Then James joined in and told everyone how Paul spent all his time with Paddy, grooming him, caring for him, giving him special food, and putting special drops into his eye twice a day.

"Paul's trying to make up for what Paddy's previous owner did to him!" Mandy explained. "And the reason he wouldn't let Paddy eat that grass, Tina, was in case it was covered in petrol fumes! So now you know," Mandy added more quietly. "And I hope all of you feel really bad for how unhappy you've made Paul feel today. Now I'm going to try and find him!"

But Mandy and James couldn't find Paul. They searched everywhere they could think of. Then they decided to go back inside the school and look.

"I suppose, in a way, I can understand how Tina made such a terrible mistake," Mandy said as she and James went inside. "You and I have got so used to Paddy that we don't notice how thin and patchy he looks!"

James nodded. "*We* just notice that he looks better every day," he agreed.

Mrs Garvie saw them walking along the corridor. "I've just had a message from Mrs Stevens," she said gently. "Paul has gone home. His mother said she'll be keeping him there for the rest of the day. She asked me to ask both of you if you'd go round after school." She smiled kindly at them. "Do you know what happened to upset Paul?"

Mandy nodded. "We do, Mrs Garvie. But it was all a terrible mistake. I think things will be much better for Paul when he comes to school tomorrow," she added.

"I just hope we can make *Paul* believe that!" said James.

When James and Mandy went round to Jasmine Cottage after school, Paul wouldn't come and talk to them.

"Tina and the others understand about Paddy now," Mandy told Paul's mother. "We're almost sure everything will be fine at school in the morning."

"I'll tell him later on," said Mrs Stevens. "He's still very upset at the moment."

"Please could you phone me later to let me know how he is?" Mandy asked.

"Yes, I'll do that, Mandy." Mrs Stevens nodded.

Later that evening, Mrs Stevens phoned Mandy and told her Paul was feeling a bit happier about things. "I think his dad and I have managed to convince him that things will be better at school now," she said. "I reckon he'll be at the end of the lane to meet you and James in the morning."

"That's good," said Mandy. "I'll phone James and tell him."

7

Apologies

"What shall we do if Paul doesn't come?" Mandy asked worriedly as soon as she met up with James the next morning.

"I don't know," James answered.

They needn't have worried, though. When they got to Paul's lane he was already waiting for them. "Tina

Cunningham phoned me last night to say she was sorry for making such a terrible mistake," he explained. "I still don't feel too good about coming to school," Paul added as they walked along. "But Dad said it would be like letting Paddy down if I didn't."

Mandy smiled. She thought Mr Stevens had said exactly the right thing!

But as they walked through the school gates, she noticed how white Paul's face had gone, and she was sure his hands were screwed into tight, worried balls inside his pockets.

When the lining-up bell rang, Mandy and James were surprised to see Mrs Todd and Mrs Black come out of the building and walk over to stand with their classes.

They were even more surprised when, after the second bell rang, the teachers led the two classes round to the front door of the school. There was a lot of giggling and whispering and breaking out of line, and nobody got told off! Mandy and James couldn't understand it at all. Until they got into the main hall . . .

Then they saw a huge poster on the school's bulletin board. It said:

Good luck to Paul Stevens and Paddy!
And to Mandy Hope and
James Hunter, who are helping Paul
to make Paddy better.

There was a border of horseshoes all around the edges of the poster. Everybody from both classes had drawn one and written their name inside it – even the teachers.

"After you'd told us all about Paul and Paddy, we all felt really bad," Tina Cunningham explained. "Then we got the idea of doing the poster to show how sorry we were. We went to Mrs Black and Mrs Todd and told them everything!"

"The school secretary phoned our parents and we all stayed late after school to do it," said Amy Fenton.

"It was an excellent idea!" Mandy laughed. "And the poster's brilliant, too!"

"It sure is," agreed James.

Paul asked if he could take the poster home to put up in Paddy's stable. "And you're all welcome to come and see Paddy sometime," he added.

When everybody yelled "Great!" and "You bet!" Mandy was so happy for Paul. She knew he'd found lots of friends in Welford.

At first break, Paul showed Mandy the presents he'd found by his place in the classroom. "Apples, carrots, a pony magazine, a hoof-pick and a bar of saddle soap!" he told her happily. "And Tina Cunningham's going to ask her mum if she can come home with me after school tomorrow. We're going to polish Paddy's tack, ready for when I can ride him!"

"That's great, Paul!" said Mandy. It would be nice if Tina and Paul became good friends, she thought. After all, Tina really cared about ponies, too!

So Paul settled down well. He had to give his new friends a progress report on Paddy every day. And Paddy was doing just fine!

Early one Saturday morning, three weeks later, Mrs Hope answered the phone to hear an anxious-sounding Paul asking if she could come and look at Paddy. "He's acting really strangely," said Paul. "I'm worried that he's got tummy ache."

"I'll be with you in ten minutes, Paul." Mrs Hope put the phone down and called to Mandy.

"Do you think it's serious, Mum?" asked Mandy as she scrambled quickly into the Land-rover.

"I don't know, love. Paul certainly sounded very worried. But we'll just have to wait and see."

When they arrived at Jasmine Cottage, Mrs Stevens and Paul were standing by the paddock gate watching Paddy. "Look at him, Mrs Hope!" said Paul, pointing to the pony.

Paddy, his dark tail stuck straight out behind him, was galloping round and round the paddock. Every so often, he slowed down a bit and gave a funny little jump in the air. Then he was off again, galloping at a tremendous pace.

"He was doing that when I first came outside and he hasn't stopped since," Paul explained. "He won't come when I whistle for him, or when I call him."

"Does that mean he hasn't had his breakfast yet?" asked Mrs Hope. Paul nodded. Mrs Hope continued. "That's OK, then, I wouldn't have felt too happy about the way he's acting if he'd eaten right beforehand. Try calling him again and see what happens."

Mandy glanced thoughtfully at her mum. She didn't sound particularly worried.

"Paddy! Paddy!" called Paul. "Come on, boy. There's a good pony."

Mandy added her voice to Paul's. Suddenly, Paddy stopped and gave a low whinny. Then he drew in his nose until it touched his chest, and stretched first one hindleg, then the other, out behind him. He tossed his broad head, then trotted towards the paddock gate.

Mrs Hope smiled down at Paul. "I think Paddy has suddenly realised just how well he's feeling," she said. Paddy whinnied again and wrinkled his muzzle as he got up close.

Mrs Hope rubbed his nose, then felt inside his mouth and ears and looked in his eyes. She climbed over the gate and stroked him all over his body and down his legs, her fingers feeling for any sign of pain or tension. Then she took a close look at his scars and the healed-up sores. "He's fine, Paul. Nothing to worry about at all."

"Oh dear," said Mrs Stevens. "So we called you out for nothing!"

"No problem," Mrs Hope told her. "Paddy was due for a visit from us today, anyway. But I think perhaps . . ." Mrs Hope smiled at Paul again, ". . . Paddy could be feeling a bit bored. It's time to give him a bit more to do during the day."

Paul looked at her, puzzled. But Mandy gave an excited squeak. She'd guessed what her mum was getting at.

"I mean, time for you to start thinking about riding Paddy!" Mrs Hope told Paul. "I would begin by just putting his saddle and bridle on two or three times today, to get him used to you doing it and to the feel of them. Then tomorrow you could ride him gently around the paddock for a while."

"Wow!" said Paul. "That's terrific news!"

"Meantime," said Mrs Hope, "give Paddy a little bit of hay to nibble at before you let him have his proper feed. He'll be hungry after all that activity and might eat his food too quickly. Then he *could* get tummy ache."

"That's why I never give Paddy very cold water," said Paul. "In case that hurts his tummy."

"You're doing everything right, Paul!" Mrs Hope reassured him. "You've only had Paddy a little over a month, but the difference in him is amazing."

"Well, I've had lots of help from everybody," said Paul. "And," he added, looking at Mandy, "I think I'm going to need more help saddling him up for the first time and . . . getting on him tomorrow to ride him! I feel really nervous about it all."

"I'm sure you'll be fine," said Mrs Hope. "Just take everything nice and easy."

"I'll go and get Paddy's grooming stuff," said Paul. "We could phone James and ask him to come over as well, Mandy. You *are* staying, aren't you?"

Mandy looked at her mum. "It's all right by me." Mrs Hope nodded. "Don't be late for lunch, though. We're meant to be going shopping this afternoon, remember?"

8

Ups and downs

"I just know I'm going to be all fingers and thumbs!" said Paul. He'd spent the last hour checking Paddy's tack and now he was about to saddle him. "It's ages since I saddled a pony," he added.

"You'll be OK, Paul," encouraged James. "I think Paddy understands what's happening. He's standing nice and still for you."

"He *is*!" agreed Mandy, climbing on to the middle rung of the gate and hanging over it to get a closer look.

Paddy moved his head forward to see what Paul was holding. He stretched his top lip away from his mouth.

"He's using his lip to feel the reins," Paul explained. "Is it OK if I put them on you, Paddy?"

Paul's fingers trembled slightly as he slipped the reins over Paddy's head and neck. But Paddy stood so patiently that Paul was soon handling everything with confidence. The pony didn't even mind when Paul slipped a thumb into the side of his mouth to put the bit in.

"Now for the saddle, Paddy," said Paul. "There's a good pony. You are standing nice and quiet, aren't you?"

Paul stepped back to look proudly at the saddled pony. "I'll only keep it on for a few minutes this time," he said. "I'll leave it on for longer after lunch."

"Hold it there!" Mr Stevens spoke quietly as he came up behind James and Mandy and started clicking a camera. "I think you and James ought to be in a photo too, Mandy," he said. "Hop over the gate and go and stand next to Paul and Paddy."

After they'd had their photo taken it was time for Mandy and James to go. But they promised Paul they'd be back the next day to watch his first proper ride!

★

"Well, here goes," said Paul, sounding nervous. He stroked Paddy's neck, then turned so he was standing with his back to the pony's head. He took the reins in his left hand and placed them just in front of the saddle. He took hold of the saddle with his right hand and put his left foot in the stirrup.

"I'm scared to do it!" said Paul, taking his foot out of the stirrup.

Paddy gave a small whinny and swung his head round to gaze at Paul.

"There! Paddy's telling you not to be so silly!" said Paul's mum. "He wants you to ride him. Just look how bright his eyes are!"

"OK, OK," muttered Paul, stroking Paddy's cheek before gently pushing the pony's head away. "I'll do it this time, Paddy. I promise."

Paul took a deep breath and put his foot in the stirrup again. This time, he followed through. He beamed down at James and

Mandy from Paddy's back, then spoke quietly to his pony and, the next minute, Paddy was 'walking on'. After a few turns around the paddock, Paul called, "I'm going to get him to trot."

Mandy heard running footsteps behind her and turned to see who was coming. It was Jane Jackson. "I was on my way home and I saw Paul and Paddy from the lane. I just *had* to come and watch!" she said.

"That pony moves really well," she added, her eyes following Paddy. "I wouldn't mind betting that he's a good little jumper. Has Paul ever done any jumping, Mrs Stevens?"

"He did a bit at the riding-school he went to before we came here," Mrs Stevens replied. "Perhaps we should set a few jumps up in the paddock," she added thoughtfully. "If Paul likes the idea, and if your mum thinks Paddy's fit enough, Mandy, we could plan it for next weekend!"

Paul loved the idea. And the next time

Mrs Hope checked Paddy over, she said he was definitely fit enough.

"Great!" said Paul. "Do you hear that, Paddy? On Saturday, we're going to try jumping. And don't worry, Mrs Hope," he added. "I won't let Paddy strain himself or anything. If he doesn't like it, we won't do it."

Mr Stevens bought some thick, round lengths of wood to use for poles and on Saturday morning Paul, Mandy, James and Jane helped him set up a series of wide-apart 'pole-jumps'. They placed each pole across two bricks about thirty centimetres off the ground.

Paul had tethered Paddy to the outside of the paddock gate and the pony kept whinnying loudly. "I'm sure he knows what this is all about!" said Paul. "Paddy's a very clever pony."

"Well, that's the last jump done," Jane told him. "Time to mount him, Paul. I'll hold the gate open for you when you're ready."

"I'll walk him round the outside of the jumps first," said Paul, "to make sure he sees them all and isn't frightened of them."

"Paddy certainly *isn't* frightened!" chuckled James. "He looks the way Blackie looks when I pick up his lead."

"Good job he doesn't leap up like Blackie, though!" Mandy joked.

Paul walked, then cantered Paddy up to each pole. Paddy soared over them easily. Jane had guessed right. Paddy *was* a really fine jumper.

"Paul's good, Mr Stevens," said Jane, after Paul and Paddy had been round the course several times. "Really good. Do you think he'd like to join our Pony Club up at the riding stables? Then he could enter the gymkhana I'm organising for the under-tens."

"I'm sure he'd love that." Mr Stevens nodded. "You ask him, Jane."

When Paul dismounted, he gave Paddy a big cuddle and told him what a good pony he was. Paddy blew into Paul's face

then rubbed his soft muzzle up and down his cheek. "I *know* you enjoyed it, Paddy!" said Paul. "But I'm going to unsaddle you now and you can have a rest."

Jane asked Paul about the gymkhana. "I could come round on Prince and we could have some mini-competitions in your paddock to get Paddy used to the idea," she said.

"I'd love you to bring Prince round," Paul said. "But I don't want to join the club or take part in a proper gymkhana, Jane."

"Whyever not, Paul?" asked Mr Stevens, sounding surprised.

"I just don't want to, that's all," mumbled Paul, turning red.

"OK." Jane sighed. "But we're having a sort of gymkhana practice tomorrow. Why don't you come up to the stables and meet the club members and their ponies, Paul?"

"The stables are awfully far away. It would be too far for Paddy just yet," said Paul.

"I'll drive you there," Mr Stevens told him.

"Thanks, Dad," said Paul. But he didn't sound very enthusiastic.

When Jane and his parents had gone, Paul glanced at Mandy and James and blurted out, "I'd love to join the club really. But Tina Cunningham told me they've got some really beautiful ponies there. Palominos and shiny, chestnut Welsh Mountain ponies. I love Paddy lots and lots, but I know he isn't beautiful. I'd hate it if anyone laughed at him or thought he looked patchy. Paddy wouldn't like it, either."

"But he doesn't look patchy any more, Paul!" said James, running his hand over Paddy's back.

"Maybe not. But his coat isn't sleek and shiny like Prince's. And it won't be as sleek as the other ponies' coats at the stable. I just know it." Paul shook his head. His answer was still "no".

★

A few days later, Jane came up to Mandy and James in the village when they were walking Blackie. "I can't understand why Paul won't join the club!" she said. "I've asked him over and over again! He seems really pleased when I take Prince round to compete against him and Paddy. I just know they'd have a marvellous time at the gymkhana."

"Maybe James and I can persuade him to join the club and to enter the gymkhana!" Mandy said determinedly. "Can't we, James?"

James nodded. But he wasn't too sure *how* they were going to do it.

"Make it soon then, Mandy," Jane said. "The entry forms have to be in by Friday. That only leaves you three days!"

By Hand

The Pony Club
Secretary

9

Problems for Mandy

When Mandy went home, she talked
things over with her mum and dad.

"Paul's scared that the Pony Club
members might laugh at Paddy!" she said.
"We all think Paddy's gorgeous, but . . ."

"Paddy isn't as handsome as most
ponies." Mr Hope nodded in agreement.

"But you know, Mandy, he *is* a perfect Exmoor."

"Is he?" Mandy asked thoughtfully. "Is he really, Dad?"

"Uh-oh!" Mrs Hope laughed. "I recognise that look on your face, Mandy Hope! What have you thought of?"

"Well, could one of you possibly find some excuse to call round at Paul's tomorrow afternoon and mention that? I think it could make a big difference to how Paul feels about Paddy."

The next day, Paul was just jumping Paddy over a double fence when Mr Hope arrived. He winked at Mandy and said he happened to be passing so he'd come to collect her. Mandy smiled happily. She could always count on her dad.

When Paul trotted over on Paddy, Mr Hope went into action. "You've worked wonders, Paul," he said. "Paddy's winter coat is going to be fantastic. It's thick and springy, and look at his tail!"

"This bit at the top looks like a fan," said Mandy.

"We call that an ice tail," Mr Hope told them. "In the native wild, on Exmoor, the tail gives protection against rain and snow. And Paddy's eyes are hooded for the same reason, aren't they, fella! You really *are* a perfect Exmoor."

"Did you hear that, Paddy?" murmured Mandy, planting a kiss on the pony's muzzle. "A *perfect* Exmoor! If you belonged to me, I'd want to show you off. I'd want everyone to see you!"

She looked at Paul. "I think it's a real shame you won't join the Pony Club!"

"Yup!" James agreed. "I'm sure none of the Pony Clubbers would laugh at a perfect Exmoor pony."

"Well, if he's as perfect as you say, maybe I will think about joining after all," said Paul.

"I think maybe ponies need *pony* friends as well as human ones!" Mandy said.

"That's right," added James. "Blackie enjoys being with other dogs. I bet Paddy would—"

"OK! OK! I'll do it!" said Paul, sliding quickly off Paddy's back. "I'll join the club *and* enter the gymkhana! Where do I get the forms from?"

"I bet Jane's got some!" said Mandy. "Have you got time to drive me up to Rose Cottage, Dad?"

"You could fill the forms in now, Paul, and one of us could post them for you on our way home," James said.

Mr Hope winked at Mandy once more. The plan had worked!

A little while later, Paul – helped by his mother, Mandy, James and Mr Hope – had filled in all the details on the forms. Mrs Stevens wrote out a cheque for the entry fee and addressed the envelope to the Pony Club Secretary.

Just then, Mr Hope's mobile phone rang. It was Mrs Forsyth, the owner of the riding stables. One of her ponies was giving birth to twin foals and needed a bit of help in delivering the second one.

"Do you want to come with me, Mandy?" Mr Hope asked.

Mandy nodded eagerly. "And I'll do better than *post* your entry form, Paul! The Pony Club's office is at the riding stables. I'll give the form to the secretary while Dad's helping with the second foal!"

When they arrived at the stables Mandy said she'd go to the Pony Club office with Paul's entry form right away. As Mandy walked, she stopped to talk to and stroke all the ponies who popped their heads over the half-doors of their stables. Their names were displayed on name-plates above the doors: Jet, Dixie, Megan, Jester, Smoky . . .

Smoky! Mandy thought. There was something strange about the beautiful grey pony. She seemed to be staring hard at nothing, and she didn't blink or move

when Mandy reached out to pet her.

"Your neck feels all tight, and it's damp and warm!" Mandy said worriedly.

Smoky's ears didn't flicker at all when Mandy spoke. They stayed forward and the pony just kept staring into space. "I think I'd better fetch somebody!" said Mandy. "Dad!"

"It looks like tetanus," Mr Hope said quietly, after he'd examined Smoky. "It's very serious, but hopefully we might just have caught it in time. I'm going to put cotton wool in her ears, because noise will upset her. I'll give her some injections and we need lots of bales of straw. We'll have to pack them all around her to stop her falling down. Move as quickly and as quietly as you can."

Mrs Forsyth, one of the stable lads and Mandy all fetched bales and helped surround Smoky with them.

"She won't want to eat," Mr Hope explained. "Chewing and swallowing will hurt too much. So try spoon-feeding her with water. I'll come back later and fix up a special drip."

"Will Smoky get better, Dad?" Mandy asked miserably, on their way home. "She looks very ill."

"She *is* very ill," Mr Hope said, nodding. "Mum or I will have to go and see her at least once a day. But I think she might make it," Mr Hope added.

★

Nearly a week went past before Mr Hope said he thought Smoky was out of danger. Mandy saw Jane Jackson that day and happily told her the good news.

"That's great!" Jane smiled. But then she frowned and said, "I thought you said you'd persuaded Paul to join the club and enter the gymkhana, Mandy. His name didn't appear in the list they published in the newspaper. Did he change his mind?"

Mandy's heart skipped a beat and her hand went to her mouth. She hadn't given the envelope to the secretary; she'd forgotten all about it! She didn't even know where she'd put it!

"I was on my way to the office with the entry forms when I saw Smoky acting strangely," she told Jane. "I must have put the envelope down somewhere when I ran for help, or when I was helping with the bales of straw. Perhaps I could go up to the riding stables and look for it. Or should I get Paul to fill in some more forms? Have you got any left?"

Jane looked worried. "It's a very strict rule that once the list of entrants has been published, no more names can be added to it," she explained.

"But Paul's name should have been on the list!" said Mandy. "He filled the forms in before the closing date. And he wrote the date on the forms. When I find the envelope, the secretary will see they were filled in on time. I'll be able to explain what happened!"

"I don't know if that would make any difference, Mandy!" Jane said. "But let's cycle up to the riding stables now. I'll help you explain everything to Miss Fletcher, the secretary. She just might be able to think of a way round things. She knows all about what happened to Smoky, so that should help!"

But it didn't help. Miss Fletcher said she was really, really sorry, but there was no way she could add Paul's name to the list of entrants – not now that the list had been in the paper. "But Mrs Stevens even wrote a cheque for the entry fee," said Mandy. "If I can just find the envelope—"

"I'm afraid Paul will have to wait for the next gymkhana," said Mrs Fletcher. "And you'd better explain what's happened to Mrs Stevens as quickly as possible, Mandy. She'll need to cancel the cheque she wrote."

"Don't worry, Mandy," said Jane. "I'll have a word with Mrs Stevens."

"I don't know *how* I'm going to tell Paul," Mandy said, as she and Jane cycled back to Welford. Her bike wobbled a bit as she lifted a hand to wipe away a tear. "I've really let him down."

"I'm sure Paul will understand," said Jane.

"But I feel like I've let Paddy down as well," said Mandy. She'd never felt so bad in all her life!

10

The gymkhana

"It doesn't matter, Mandy. *Really* it doesn't!" said Paul when Mandy told him what had happened. "Getting help for Smoky was more important than handing my entry forms in!"

"Yes, it was. But I should have remembered your forms afterwards!"

Mandy sighed unhappily.

"Listen, Mandy," said Paul. "I can still join the club. There's no problem there. And that's the important thing. Paddy will still be able to have the pony friends you talked about!"

Mandy nodded. But she still felt terrible.

James tried to think of ways to make her feel better. On the day before the gymkhana, he asked her to help him give Blackie a bath! Mandy wore her new wellies so Blackie couldn't make her feet all wet! And just for a little while Mandy didn't feel so bad. But then they took Blackie for a walk and they met Jane Jackson.

Jane told Mandy she was going to try to organise another gymkhana quite soon. "Maybe a special New Year one," she said.

"But New Year's ages away!" said Mandy. "Besides, it was *this* one that would have been so special for Paul."

"Why would it have been so special?" Jane asked gently.

Mandy gulped. "Well, even though Dad told Paul that Paddy's a perfect Exmoor pony, I'm sure Paul still worries about Paddy looking a bit different from other ponies. They'd have done well at the gymkhana. I'm sure they'd have won at least one prize."

James nodded. "And everyone would have clapped and cheered, and Paul would have been so proud of the pony he saved!"

"*James!*" shrieked Mandy. "You've just made me think of the most brilliant idea! We'll have to ask Dad about it first, and then make sure Paul comes to the gymkhana. Come on, we've got to go to Animal Ark!"

Mandy, Paul and James watched all the gymkhana events together. Mandy kept glancing anxiously round to see if her mum or dad had arrived.

Mr Hope had been chosen to give out the prizes at the end of the gymkhana.

He had been called out just before they'd left home, but told Mandy that he would definitely be back in time for prize-giving.

Now they were on the last event and Mandy couldn't see him anywhere!

"The strawberry roan pony is going to win," shouted Paul. "He's fantastic! I hoped he'd come first and . . . and . . . yes! He's done it!"

"And it'll soon be time for the prizes to be awarded," Mandy whispered to James, who was on her other side.

"Here's your dad now, Mandy!" said James a few minutes later. He pointed to a figure running hard across the field towards the bales of piled-up hay that were to be the presentation platform.

So the prize-giving began. There was lots of cheering and clapping and Mandy cheered loudest of all because she was so excited about what was going to happen at the end.

When the last winner had walked away with a rosette, Mr Hope stepped forward again and called for silence. "I now have a very special announcement to make and a very special rosette to present!"

He looked down to where Mandy, James and Paul were standing. Mandy's eyes sparkled as she gazed at her dad and she heard James take a deep, expectant breath.

"We have with us today," said Mr Hope, "somebody who's devoted a lot of time, care and attention – and *love* – to a pony who needed all those things more than most ponies do! I'm talking about Paul Stevens, who's given Paddy, a pony from the rescue sanctuary, a happy and loving home."

Mr Hope held up his hands to stop the applause. "Circumstances prevented Paul from entering the gymkhana," he said. "But I'd like Paul to come up to receive this special rosette because Paul's friends, especially Paddy, think he deserves a prize!"

Paul looked from Mandy to James in

astonishment. James thumped him on the back and Mandy laughed happily. Then she and James took hold of Paul's arms and propelled him to the platform to receive his rosette.

When the cheering died down, Jane Jackson stepped forward. "And I've also got a special announcement to make," she said. She beckoned to Paul.

Mr Hope reached under the table the prizes had been on. Smiling, he passed Jane a hard riding hat. Jane passed it to Paul.

Paul was puzzled. "But I've already got a riding hat," he said.

"It's *your* hat, Paul!" Jane told him. "Put it on, then go over to the ring."

Then Jane moved closer to the microphone. "Listen, everybody," she said. "Paul Stevens and Paddy are going to lead the other winners round the ring in a special Pony Parade! Go on, Paul!" she laughed. "Your mum and dad are waiting by the ring with Paddy!"

"They *can't* be," said Paul. "Paddy's in his paddock. I said goodbye to him just before I left to meet James and Mandy."

"They are, Paul. Truly!" said Jane. "Now, off you go. Or don't you want Paddy to have place of honour in the parade?" she added, teasingly.

"I can't believe it! I just can't believe it," said Paul as he, Mandy, James and Mr Hope walked towards the ring. "I mean, how did Paddy get here? We haven't got a horse box. Dad had to hire one when we went to the sanctuary."

"My dad borrowed one!" Mandy chuckled, squeezing Mr Hope's arm hard. "We fixed it all up yesterday afternoon!"

"I don't know what to say," said Paul, shaking his head. "I feel like I'm dreaming!"

"Paddy knows it's for real," said James, pointing to where the pony was standing with Mr and Mrs Stevens. "He's spotted you coming, Paul. He's pulling at the reins trying to get to you!"

Paul gave a loud whoop of joy and hurried forward to throw his arms round Paddy's neck. Then, grinning happily at his mum and dad, Paul fixed the rosette to Paddy's bridle.

A few seconds later they all watched as Paul mounted Paddy, then trotted him into the ring. As he got close to one of the Palomino ponies, Paddy stopped. He stretched his upper lip and used it to explore the Palomino's mane and ears.

"Look!" shouted someone in the crowd. "That pony is smiling at the Palomino!"

Paul beamed round at everybody, patted Paddy, then said huskily, "Walk on, boy."

Paddy flicked his tail and walked on to take his place at the front of the parade.

Mandy felt so happy for Paul! James grinned at her, then jumped up and down with delight as everyone started clapping and cheering.

There were quite a few kids from school in the crowd. They set up a chant: "Paul and Paddy! Paul and Paddy! Paul and Paddy!" And before long everyone joined in the chant.

Paul smiled and waved and the chant became louder still. The pony clubbers riding behind Paul and Paddy halted their ponies and joined in. Paul laughed aloud and stroked Paddy's neck. He looked so proud of his pony!

Paul and Paddy will have even more new friends after today, thought Mandy as she watched them go once round the ring on their own.

Then Paul called to the other riders

to follow him and he urged Paddy into a brisk trot. This time, when Paul rode Paddy to where Mandy and James were standing, the Exmoor pony whinnied loudly.

Mandy gave an enormous, contented sigh. She was sure that whinny was just for them!

LUCY DANIELS

Animal Ark™

Guinea-pig
Gang

**Hodder
Children's
Books**

A division of Hachette Children's Books

Special thanks to Helen Magee

Text copyright © 1997 Working Partners Ltd.
Created by Working Partners Limited, London W6 0QT
Original series created by Ben M. Baglio
Illustrations copyright © 1997 Paul Howard

First published as a single volume in Great Britain in 1997
by Hodder Children's Books

Contents

1

Pet Day at school

"Oh, Pam, you *are* lucky to have such a beautiful pet!" said Mandy Hope. She gazed at the reddish-brown guinea-pig, scampering around the classroom floor. "Aren't you gorgeous, Ginny!"

Ginny, the guinea-pig, was surrounded by a wide ring of children, sitting cross-legged on the floor. Every so often she would scurry up to one of them, twitching her whiskers and snuffling.

"You think *all* animals are gorgeous," James Hunter said to Mandy. His eyes were shining behind his glasses.

"And *you* like animals almost as much as Mandy does," said Pam Stanton to James.

Mandy and James grinned at Pam. Mandy's parents were both vets in the little village of Welford. Their surgery was called Animal Ark and it was at the back of their stone cottage.

There were always a lot of animals coming in and out of Animal Ark. Mandy loved it. Mandy thought animals were the most important thing in the world. James was her best friend. He had a black Labrador called Blackie.

Ginny ran across the floor and stopped in front of a girl with short red-brown hair.

"She likes you, Lisa," Pam said as Ginny

sat back on her haunches and looked at Lisa with her bright button eyes.

Lisa Glover was in James's class. She stretched out a hand gently. The little guinea-pig sniffed at it, then put one tiny paw into Lisa's palm. She lifted Ginny up and stroked her fur.

"Lisa thinks Ginny is gorgeous too," said James.

Mandy smiled. "Look!" she said. "Lisa's hair is almost the same colour as Ginny's coat."

Lisa looked up at Mrs Todd and Mrs Black. The two teachers had organised a pet afternoon every Friday of that term. "This is the best Pet Day yet," she said to them. "I love guinea-pigs."

"I think we've had a very successful session," Mrs Todd agreed. "Ginny has been very well-behaved and I'm sure we're all very grateful to Pam for all the information she's given us." Mrs Todd was Mandy's teacher at Welford Village School.

Lisa walked across to Pam and held Ginny out to her. Pam took Ginny in her arms and gave her a cuddle.

"Stay where you are until Pam has put Ginny in her cage," Mrs Todd said. "We don't want our guinea-pig guest to get frightened."

"Let's hope your projects are as successful as Pam's talk," Mrs Black joked. "And I hope everyone is going to enter their pets for the best-kept pet competition at the Welford Show.

We certainly seem to have a lot of expert pet owners here in Welford Village."

James was in the class below Mandy at school. Mrs Black, his teacher, often joined up with Mrs Todd for projects. Each week of that term one of the pupils would bring in their pet and explain how to look after it. Lots of them had already decided to enter their pets at the Welford Show, which took place once a year.

"This is a brilliant way to spend Friday afternoons," Mandy said, tickling Ginny under the chin. "I'm going to do a drawing of Ginny for the project."

"And I'll do a food chart for her," James added.

"I'll help you," Gary Roberts said.

"And me," Jill Redfern offered.

The two classes buzzed with excitement as they planned their projects. Pam put Ginny back in her cage and the little animal began grooming herself. Ginny had a smooth reddish-brown coat and bright black eyes.

"Guinea-pigs keep themselves really clean, don't they?" Richard Tanner said. "Just like cats." Richard had a Persian cat called Duchess.

Pam nodded. "You don't have to bath them," she said. "But sometimes I brush Ginny's coat just because I like doing it – and Ginny likes it too."

James had started a list. "I've put down crushed oats and guinea-pig mixture," he said. "What else does Ginny eat, Pam?"

"She needs lots of greens and roots," Pam said. "And don't forget hay and water."

"Hay?" asked Peter Foster.

Pam nodded. "Guinea-pigs love it," she said. "A handful or two each day should be enough. If there's any left over the guinea-pig will use it for bedding. You have to make sure there aren't any thistles in it, though. They can hurt the guinea-pig's throat."

"What a lot there is to remember," said Amy Fenton.

"You get used to it," Pam said. "*You* don't forget how to look after Minnie, *do* you?"

Amy shook her head. "Oh, no," she said. "I couldn't do that." Minnie was Amy's white mouse.

"It seems to me you all look after your pets very well," Mrs Todd said. "I can't imagine Peter forgetting to give Timmy his dinner."

Peter grinned. "Timmy would remind me!" he said. Timmy was a cairn terrier and just about the naughtiest dog in Welford.

"Whose turn is it next week?" Mrs Black asked.

"Mine," said Jill. "I'm bringing Toto." Toto was Jill's tortoise.

"Who wants to do the session after that?" asked Mrs Todd.

A forest of hands shot up into the air.

"Can I bring Gertie?" Gary asked.

"I could bring Blackie," said James.

"Let's have Blackie that week and Gertie the garter-snake the week after," Mrs Black suggested.

James flushed with pleasure.

Gary was pleased too. "Great," he said. "I'm going to read as much as I can about snakes before then."

"Who else has a pet?" asked Mrs Todd. "We want all of your pets to visit us."

"What about you, Lisa?" Mrs Black asked.

Lisa flushed. "I haven't got a pet," she said.

"Oh, what a shame," said Sarah Drummond. "You should get a puppy. James and I have both got black Labradors. We got them from the same litter."

"Mine is called Blackie," said James.

"And mine is Sooty," said Sarah. "He's gorgeous."

Lisa bit her lip. "I mean I don't have a pet *yet*," she said. "In fact I'm getting a guinea-pig next week."

Pam smiled widely. "A guinea-pig!" she said. "That's terrific. What kind?"

"Oh, a really special one," Lisa said. "It's called a Tort and White. It's got black, white and red markings. It isn't just an ordinary guinea-pig."

Pam looked at Ginny. "I don't think *Ginny* is ordinary either," she said.

"But this is a cavy," said Lisa.

"What's that?" James asked.

"It's a pedigree guinea-pig," Lisa answered. "A pure-bred."

"Lots of people in school have guinea-pigs," Jill said.

"That's right," said Pam. "We've even got a guinea-pig gang. There are five of us. We all have guinea-pigs and we meet up every week with our pets to play with them and talk about them. You can join if you like."

"You can bring your guinea-pig to school and let us see it," said Mandy.

"And you can bring it to visit Ginny," added Pam.

Lisa flushed even more. "Oh, no," she said. "I couldn't do that. I wouldn't be allowed to. It's a *pedigree*."

The bell for the end of school rang and Lisa turned away.

"Well," said Pam. "It looks like Ginny isn't good enough to mix with a *pedigree* guinea-pig!"

"She didn't mean it like that," Mandy said.

Pam snorted. "I think Lisa Glover is really snooty," she said. "You don't have to be a pedigree guinea-pig to be beautiful."

Pam picked up Ginny's cage and walked towards the classroom door.

"Uh-oh!" said James. "Pam is really upset. Lisa shouldn't have said that."

Mandy frowned. "I think Lisa was upset as well," she said.

"What about?" James asked.

"I don't know," she said. "But I got the feeling she was unhappy about something."

"She wasn't very nice to Pam about Ginny," James replied.

Mandy shook her head. "But Lisa *loved* Ginny," she said. "Didn't you see the way she held her? And she was really interested in everything Pam was saying about looking after guinea-pigs."

"So why was she so snooty about her pedigree guinea-pig?" said James.

Mandy frowned. "I'm not sure," she said. "But I know one thing. Lisa didn't care about Ginny not being a pedigree. She really liked her."

"Mmm," said James. "Well, I thought she was snooty." He grinned. "Are you coming round to my house tonight? I've taught Blackie a new trick and I want you to see it. He loves showing off."

Mandy laughed. "Don't tell me," she said. "He can sit still for two minutes!"

"No," said James. "I don't think Blackie will ever be able to do that. But he *can* beg for a biscuit. You should see him catch it!"

"Are you going to put him in for the Welford Show?" asked Mandy. "There's a really big pet section this year."

James shook his head. "Not this time," he said. "But maybe next year – if I can get him to walk to heel, and sit, and come when he's called."

"Gran is going to have a home-baking stall at the Show," Mandy added.

"Is she going to make ginger biscuits for it?" James asked.

Mandy nodded. "And doughnuts."

"Do you think your gran would let me help on the stall?" said James.

"Only if you promised not to eat all the biscuits," Mandy replied. "Now, what are you going to say at the pets session?"

Mandy and James discussed James's talk all the way home. But, at the back of her mind, Mandy was still wondering what had upset Lisa.

2

Carla the cavy

"Guess what?" Mandy said as she came into the kitchen of Animal Ark the following Wednesday after school.

"You put your schoolbag away, instead of leaving it in the hall for me to trip over?" Mr Hope replied, his dark eyes twinkling.

Mandy grinned. "Nope!" she said. "Something much more exciting than that. Do you give up?"

Mr and Mrs Hope nodded.

"Lisa Glover has got her guinea-pig," Mandy said, plonking herself down at the table.

"The Tort and White?" said Mr Hope. "They're very unusual. I'd love to see it."

"I knew you would," said Mandy. "So I told her she could bring it round tonight for a check-up. Is that all right?"

Mr Hope laughed. "Ask your mum," he said. "She's the one doing evening surgery."

Mrs Hope shook her head. She had bright-red hair tied in a ponytail. "Mandy, you should have checked with Jean." Jean Knox was Animal Ark's receptionist.

"Oh, you aren't all booked up, are you?" asked Mandy. "I thought it would be OK."

Mrs Hope shook her head again. "I *suppose* I can squeeze in another appointment," she said. "But in future ask your friends to go through Jean."

"I will," said Mandy. Then she looked worried. "What if it's an emergency?"

"An emergency is different," Mr Hope said. "We'll always see an animal in an emergency. There isn't anything wrong with the guinea-pig, is there?"

Mandy shook her head. "No, but Lisa's mum thought it should have a check-up."

"Very wise," said Mrs Hope. She looked at Mandy. "And the answer is yes – so long as you don't get in the way."

"Yes, what?" asked Mandy, puzzled.

"Yes, you *can* come into the surgery while I examine the guinea-pig," said Mrs Hope.

"Yippee!" said Mandy. "That's great, Mum."

Lisa and her sister, Jennifer, brought the guinea-pig into surgery that evening in a brand-new cage. Jennifer was thirteen, five years older than Lisa. The sisters weren't at all alike. Lisa had short reddish-brown hair and dark eyes. Jennifer had long fair hair and blue eyes. Nobody would ever guess they were sisters.

Mandy looked eagerly at the little guinea-pig. She drew in her breath in surprise. She had *never* seen a guinea-pig like it before!

"This is Carla," Jennifer said, putting the cage down on the examination table.

"Oh, she's gorgeous," Mandy said. "Just look at her markings, Mum!"

"She's a Tortoiseshell and White," Jennifer said.

"That's quite a big name for a little animal," Mrs Hope said, smiling.

The guinea-pig was marked with square patches of red, black and white. Looked at from above, she looked like she was wearing a check coat.

"She really is beautiful," Mrs Hope said. "Tort and whites are so difficult to breed. You've got a very good specimen here, Lisa."

"They *are* difficult to breed," Jennifer agreed. "That's why they're so special and *that's* why I wanted her."

Mandy looked curiously at Jennifer and Lisa. Lisa hadn't said a word. Jennifer was acting as if Carla was *her* guinea-pig. Maybe Carla was a family pet – not just Lisa's.

"She's very healthy as well," Mrs Hope said, putting Carla back in her cage. "You shouldn't have any problems there at all."

"Thanks, Mrs Hope," Lisa said. "I'm glad you like her."

"Nobody could help liking her," Mrs Hope said. "She's a beauty."

Jennifer nodded as Mrs Hope went to the sink to wash her hands. "Of course she is," she said. "She's a prize-winner."

The three girls trooped out of the surgery.

"Has Carla won prizes?" Mandy asked, surprised.

"Not yet," said Jennifer. "But she will. The Welford Show is at the end of next month. There's a guinea-pig competition this year. I'm going to put Carla in for the pure-bred section – that's for pedigree guinea-pigs. She's bound to win a prize."

"*You* are?" asked Mandy. "But I thought Carla was Lisa's guinea-pig."

Jennifer looked at her little sister. "Oh, no," she said. "Carla is mine. She was a birthday present. And I've told Lisa she isn't to go messing around with her."

"I only want to play with her," Lisa explained.

"Well, you can't," said Jennifer. "She's mine. And I don't want her all fussed over. She's got to look her best for the show if she's going to win a prize."

"Guinea-pigs like company," Mandy said carefully to Jennifer. "They don't mind being fussed over. They enjoy it."

Jennifer looked down her nose at Mandy. "You're only a year older than Lisa," she said. "What do *you* know?"

"Mandy knows lots about animals," Lisa said. "She knows more than you do."

Mandy looked at Lisa in surprise and Lisa blushed.

"Just because her parents are vets doesn't mean she knows everything," Jennifer said.

"Of course not," said Mandy. "I don't know all that much about animals. But I do like them."

"Are you saying I don't?" asked Jennifer, tossing her hair back. "I think Carla is beautiful. That's why I wanted

her for my birthday. Nobody else I know has got such a pretty pet."

Jennifer turned round and marched off. Mandy looked at Lisa.

"Sorry about Jennifer," Lisa said to Mandy. "Ever since she turned thirteen she thinks she's all grown up and I'm just a little kid."

"It really is a shame that she won't let you play with Carla," Mandy said. "Guinea-pigs *love* being played with."

"I know," said Lisa. "But Jennifer won't listen. She doesn't know the first thing about guinea-pigs and she won't let me touch Carla. She only wanted Carla because she thought she looked nice. But that isn't right. You can't have a pet just because you think it looks nice."

Mandy bit her lip. Lisa was really upset.

"Once Jennifer gets to know Carla she'll like her for all sorts of reasons," Mandy said. "Not just because she looks nice."

"I hope so," said Lisa. "Do you know that she couldn't make up her mind whether she wanted a personal stereo or a guinea-pig for her birthday?"

"But she *did* choose to have a guinea-pig," said Mandy.

"Only because Carla was so special," Lisa said. "If *I* had one I wouldn't care if it was a pedigree or not."

Jennifer's voice floated back to them. "Come on, Lisa!" she called.

Lisa gave Mandy a quick smile and turned to go. "See you," she said.

Mandy watched as she walked off after her sister.

Poor Lisa. Imagine having an animal at home and not even being allowed to play with it. No wonder she was unhappy!

3

Guinea-pigs galore

Next day at school, Mandy told Pam all about Jennifer and Carla.

"People like Jennifer shouldn't be allowed to have pets," Pam said.

Mandy shook her head. "I don't think Jennifer *means* to be unkind to Carla. It's just that she doesn't know anything about looking after guinea-pigs."

"She should have been in our class last Friday," James said. "Then she would know all about them. You were really good, Pam."

Pam blushed. "Thanks," she replied. "But I can't understand why Jennifer would even want a guinea-pig when she can't be bothered to find out about them."

"She wanted Carla because she's so unusual," Mandy explained.

"She sounds beautiful," James agreed.

"I've never seen a guinea-pig like her before," said Mandy. "She's perfect." Then she frowned. "It's just that her owner isn't."

"Shh!" said James. "Here comes Lisa."

They turned as Lisa came through the school gates. She was walking with her head down, feet scuffing.

"Hi, Lisa!" Mandy said. "What's up?"

Lisa shrugged. "Nothing really," she said. "By the way, thanks for trying to talk to Jennifer yesterday."

"I don't suppose she's changed her mind about letting you play with Carla?" Mandy asked.

Lisa shook her head. "I wouldn't mind if Jennifer played with her. But she doesn't. Poor Carla is getting so bored."

"That isn't *your* fault," James said. "You *want* to play with her. It's Jennifer that says you can't."

"That's wrong," said Mandy. "Pets aren't possessions."

"Try telling that to Jennifer," Lisa said.

Pam put her head on one side. "How would you like to come and visit Ginny?" she asked.

Lisa's face lit up. "Could I?" she said. "That would be great."

"Ginny would love it," Pam said. "Come on Friday, after school. That's when the Guinea-Pig Gang meets."

"You told me about that before," said Lisa. "Who's in it?"

"There are five of us," Pam said. "Robbie Taylor, Kate Fletcher, Ross Jarvis, Zoe Adams and me. We all have guinea-pigs and we take turns meeting at each other's house once a week. The guinea-pigs really enjoy it. So do we. It's my turn this week."

"I'd love to come," said Lisa. "Thanks, Pam."

"You two could come as well," Pam said to Mandy and James.

"But we don't have guinea-pigs," said Mandy.

154

Pam laughed. "Oh, that's all right," she said. "You can be honorary members!"

The bell rang for the start of school and they made their way towards their classes. Lisa and Pam were chatting about the Guinea-pig Gang.

"Lisa looks a lot happier now," James said to Mandy.

Mandy smiled. "I think Pam's Guinea-pig Gang will really cheer her up," she said. "And me too! I'm really looking forward to Friday. Jill is doing her talk about Toto *and* we're going to see the Guinea-pig Gang."

Mandy and James were still talking about Toto the tortoise when they arrived at Pam's house.

"Imagine hibernating all winter," James said. "I think I'd rather have a year-round pet like Blackie."

Lisa came running down the road. They waited for her and walked up the front path together.

"Hi," said Pam, opening the door. "Come and see the guinea-pigs."

They went through the house and out into the back garden. Ross, Robbie, Zoe and Kate were there already with their guinea-pigs. The pets were scampering around in two big cardboard boxes.

"Why have you got two boxes?" James asked.

"Because we don't want to have any baby guinea-pigs," Pam said. She pointed at one box. "These are the boys – Micky and Scamp."

"And these are the girls – Ginny, Brownie and Muffin," said Ross.

"Oh, they're gorgeous!" said Lisa, kneeling down to watch the guinea-pigs. "Look at them playing."

Ross had a short-haired black guinea-pig called Micky. Zoe and Kate both had rough-haired cross-breeds, while Robbie's guinea-pig was a long-haired tan-coloured boar.

"That's Scamp," Robbie said.

"He looks lovely," Lisa said. "But he must be awfully hard work with that long coat."

Robbie grinned. "I have to brush him every day," he said. "His coat gets tangled if I don't. But I don't mind. I like grooming him."

Lisa put out her hand and stroked Scamp's coat. "What do you use?" she asked.

"An ordinary hairbrush," Robbie said. "But sometimes, if his coat gets really tangled, I have to snip the knots out."

"I use a baby hairbrush to groom Muffin," Zoe said.

Pam picked Ginny up and gave her a cuddle. She seemed worried.

"Is Ginny all right?" Kate asked.

Pam frowned. "I don't know," she said. "She looks OK, but she isn't running about as much as usual."

"She *does* seem a little tired," Mandy said to Pam.

Pam nodded. "She was all right this

morning," she replied. "But she didn't eat very well yesterday. I'm a bit worried about her. She's usually so lively."

"Why don't you bring her round to Animal Ark?" Mandy suggested. "You could phone for an appointment."

Pam nodded. "I'll bring her tomorrow if she isn't any better," she said. "It just isn't like Ginny not to want to eat."

"Hey, look at Muffin and Brownie!" Ross said.

They all looked. The two guinea-pigs were circling each other and making little darting movements.

"They look as if they're dancing," James said, laughing.

"Is there a guinea-pig dancing competition at the Welford Show?" Zoe asked. "We could enter them for it!"

"I thought I might enter Scamp in the guinea-pig competition," Robbie said. "*If* I can keep his coat untangled," he added.

Everybody started talking about the

Welford Show, but Mandy noticed that Pam kept looking at Ginny. She was obviously very worried.

Ginny wasn't better on Saturday morning. The phone rang at Animal Ark as Mandy was helping her mum clear the breakfast things away.

"That was Pam Stanton," Mr Hope explained, poking his head round the kitchen door. "She's bringing Ginny round in half an hour."

Mandy put a pile of plates on the draining-board. "Is Ginny worse?" she asked.

"She's still not eating," said Mr Hope.

"I hope it isn't anything serious," Mandy said.

Mrs Hope smiled at her. "Don't you go getting all worried," she said. "She probably only needs her teeth clipped. Sometimes guinea-pigs' teeth grow too long to let them eat properly."

But Mandy couldn't help worrying when she knew an animal was unwell.

★　★　★

It seemed like ages before Pam and her mother arrived with Ginny.

"Well, well, what have we here?" Mr Hope said, as he lifted the little animal out of her cage.

Simon, the practice nurse, laid a fresh sheet of paper on the examination table and Mr Hope put Ginny down on it.

Mandy and Pam watched anxiously. Mr Hope felt Ginny's throat gently, then put his thumbs on either side of her jaw. The guinea-pig opened her mouth.

"What's wrong with her?" asked Mrs Stanton.

"Is it serious?" Pam added, looking worried.

Mr Hope looked at Pam and smiled. "I don't think it's too serious," he said. "Her teeth are all right but her throat seems to be quite painful. I'm not surprised she hasn't been eating."

"What are you going to do, Dad?" Mandy asked.

Mr Hope settled Ginny in one hand and stroked her with the other.

"First I'm going to have to put this little lady to sleep," he said. He looked at Mrs Stanton. "I'll need your permission. You'll have to sign a consent form."

"Anything you say," Mrs Stanton said. "Does she need an operation?"

Mr Hope nodded. "Just a tiny one," he said. "It looks as if she's got an abscess in her throat."

"Then we'd better get it seen to," Mrs Stanton said.

"Jean will give you the form," Mr Hope explained.

Mrs Stanton nodded. "You do what you have to do," she said. "I know Ginny will be safe with you."

"How would Ginny get an abscess?" asked Mandy, as Mrs Stanton went out.

"Mostly it's caused by thistles in the hay," Mr Hope said. "You have to be really careful to clean out any thistles before you put the hay in the cage."

"But I'm always careful," said Pam, her face pale. "I must have missed one. Oh, poor Ginny. Can you help her?"

"It doesn't look too bad," said Mr Hope. "But you two girls will have to wait outside."

Mandy bit her lip. Waiting was always the difficult part.

"Come on," said Simon. "The sooner we get started, the sooner it'll be over."

Mandy and Pam went out into the waiting-room. Pam looked back nervously as Simon shut the door behind them.

"Now, don't worry so much, Pam," Mrs Stanton said. She was standing at Jean's desk. There was an official-looking form in front of her.

"I can't help it," Pam said.

"Why don't you go and have something to drink while your mum and I do the paperwork?" Jean Knox suggested.

Mandy smiled at her. "Good idea, Jean," she said. "Will you call us when Dad has finished?"

Jean nodded. Her glasses fell off her nose and bounced at the end of their chain. "I'll let you know as soon as I hear anything," she said. "Now off you go."

Mandy led Pam through to the kitchen.

"Don't worry," she said as she poured out two glasses of juice. "Dad will make Ginny better."

Pam looked at her. "I can't help it," she said. "If anything happened to Ginny I don't know what I'd do. And it's my fault. I must have left a thistle in her hay."

"Anybody could do that," said Mandy.

Pam shook her head. "And to think I was saying things about Lisa's sister," she said. "*I* can't even look after Ginny properly."

"That isn't true," said Mandy. "No pet could have a better owner."

Pam looked at her. "Do you really think so?" she asked.

Mandy nodded. "I think you should enter Ginny in the guinea-pig competition at the Welford Show," she said. "I'm sure she'll win."

"If she gets better," said Pam.

"*When* she gets better," Mandy said firmly.

Pam smiled. "Thanks, Mandy," she said. "It really helps having you here waiting with me."

It was about ten minutes later when Jean put her head round the kitchen door. Mrs Stanton was behind her.

"Do you want to see the patient?" Jean asked.

Mandy and Pam jumped off their chairs and dashed through the door. "Is she all right?" Pam asked.

Jean beamed. "Right as rain, according to Simon," she said. "But she's still a bit drowsy."

"You go first, Pam," Mrs Stanton said.

The girls pushed the surgery door open and Pam went to the examination table. Ginny looked very small and sleepy.

"Can I pick her up?" asked Pam.

Mr Hope nodded. "Just don't touch her neck or throat," he said. "She'll be a bit tender for a day or two. But she's a fine, healthy guinea-pig."

"So she'll get better?" said Pam.

Simon grinned. "Of course she will," he said. "She's fit and strong. She's been very well looked after."

Pam cuddled Ginny very gently. "I'm so pleased," she said.

"I want to keep her here overnight,"

said Mr Hope. "But she can go back home tomorrow. Just make sure she gets plenty of tender loving care."

"Oh, I will," said Pam. "I'll watch out for thistles from now on."

"What about the show?" said Mandy. "Are you going to enter her for the guinea-pig competition? If I were a judge I'd vote for her."

"Then I will," said Pam. "And I'll make sure she's the best-kept guinea-pig in the whole world!"

4

Carla in trouble

Pam came to collect Ginny on Sunday.

"Remember, no thistles," Mr Hope said as he handed the little animal over.

Pam put Ginny gently in her cage. "I promise," she said. "I've told the rest of the Guinea-pig Gang that they have to be careful too."

"Good for you," said Mr Hope.

"Do you think Jennifer would join the Guinea-pig Gang?" Mandy asked Pam.

Pam shook her head. "I think Jennifer would think she was too grown up," she said. "But we could ask Lisa to mention it to her."

"Let's do that," said Mandy. "We'll ask her at school first thing tomorrow."

But when Mandy and James mentioned the idea, Lisa shook her head. "I've already told her about the Guinea-pig Gang," she said. "Jennifer says that's just for kids and their pets – not for pedigree guinea-pigs."

"But Carla is a pet too," said James.

"Jennifer only cares about her winning a prize at the show," said Lisa. "She's already started moaning about having to look after Carla and what a lot of work it is."

"Won't she let you help?" asked Mandy.

Lisa shook her head. "She won't let me near her," she said. "And I'm getting really worried. Carla's moping and she isn't looking nearly as healthy as she did when Jennifer got her. She certainly isn't going to be at her best for the Show."

"Jennifer won't like that," said James.

"If Carla doesn't win a prize, Jennifer won't want her at *all*," said Lisa.

Mandy bit her lip. "We've got to do something about this," she said.

"But what?" asked James. "Carla is Jennifer's guinea-pig."

Mandy frowned. "I'm beginning to think Pam was right," she said. "I don't think Jennifer should have a guinea-pig if she won't look after it properly."

"I'll try talking to her again," said Lisa. "Not that she ever listens to me — but I'll try."

Mandy and James were very busy for the rest of the week. James rehearsed his talk every day and Mandy tried to get Blackie to sit while James spoke. But every time the Labrador heard his name he jumped up, wagging his tail in delight.

"Try to do the talk without saying that word," said Mandy on the way to school on Friday afternoon.

"What word?" said James.

"Blackie," Mandy said.

Blackie gave a short bark and jumped up, licking Mandy's face.

Mandy burst out laughing. "It's no good, James," she said. "You'll just have to explain to everyone that Blackie is a very energetic dog."

"Lively," said James, grinning.

"Full of fun," Mandy agreed.

"Disobedient," James said regretfully.

Mandy didn't hear. "Look!" she said. "There's Lisa. She's upset about something."

Lisa was standing by the school gates, waiting for Mandy and James. She looked close to tears.

"What's the matter?" Mandy asked.

"Mum says Jennifer has to get rid of Carla," Lisa said.

"What?" said Mandy.

"But why?" James asked.

Blackie nudged Lisa's hand with his nose and she knelt down and put her arms round his neck.

"Mum says Jennifer isn't looking after Carla," she went on. "And she's right. Poor little Carla. Her fur has started to come out and she's scratching badly. Jennifer says she won't be fit to enter into the Welford Show."

"So what is she going to do with her?" Mandy asked, horrified.

"Mum says we have to bring Carla into

Animal Ark," Lisa said. "Honestly, you should see her. She looks terrible."

"Bring her round tonight," Mandy said. "If you get there early enough Mum or Dad will be able to see Carla straight away."

"But we haven't got an appointment," said Lisa.

Mandy set her lips in a firm line. "That doesn't matter," she said. "This sounds like an emergency!"

Mandy could hardly think about anything else all afternoon. Even James's talk didn't take her mind off Carla's problems.

"That was really excellent, James," Mrs Todd said when he had finished. "Blackie is such a charmer. He's full of fun, isn't he?"

James smiled and looked at Mandy. "That's what we think," he said.

Mandy smiled back at him, but she was anxious to get home to tell her parents about Carla.

"You were terrific," she said to James.

James nodded. "But you're thinking about Carla, aren't you?" he said. "So am I."

Mandy smiled properly this time. That was one of the good things about James. He always understood how worried she got when an animal was in trouble.

Jennifer and Lisa came round to Animal Ark just before surgery opening time.

"I'm certainly glad you brought Carla in," Mrs Hope said after she had examined the guinea-pig.

Mandy looked at poor Carla. Her beautiful check coat was sticking up in tufts and she had big bare patches all over her.

"What on earth is the matter with her?" Jennifer asked.

Mrs Hope smiled. "Nothing too dreadful," she said. "She's got mites. It looks a lot worse than it actually is."

"What are mites?" Lisa asked.

"They're tiny little creatures that burrow under a guinea-pig's skin," Mrs Hope said. "They must be making poor Carla very itchy. That's why she's scratching so much and losing her fur."

"Ugh!" said Jennifer. "Mites! That's horrible."

"It certainly is – for Carla," Mrs Hope said gently.

Jennifer went a bit red. "Look, Mrs Hope," she said, "I don't really think I want a guinea-pig any more. I didn't realise how much *work* it would be. Mum says I should try and find Carla another home. Can you help?"

"But you can't just give Carla away," Lisa said to Jennifer.

"She's my guinea-pig, not yours," Jennifer replied.

Mrs Hope looked down at Carla. Mandy held her breath. What was going to happen?

"Why don't you leave her here at Animal Ark with us until we get rid of the mites?" Mrs Hope said. "Then we can think about what to do with her."

"All right," said Jennifer. "Only, don't ask me to touch her. Mites! Yuck!"

Mrs Hope looked at Mandy and Lisa. They were trying really hard not to say anything to Jennifer.

"Maybe keeping pets isn't your thing," Mrs Hope said to Jennifer.

Jennifer took a step back from poor, scruffy-looking Carla. "I think you're right," she said. "And Mum thinks so too." She sighed. "I wish I'd got a personal stereo for my birthday instead of a guinea-pig. It would be a lot less trouble. Still, if you could help find a home for her that would be all right."

"Won't you miss her?" Lisa asked Jennifer.

Jennifer wrinkled her nose. "I won't miss all that cleaning out and stuff," she said. "Pets are a lot of work."

"But you could try to like it for Carla's sake," Lisa pleaded. "Can't you try just one more time?"

Jennifer shook her head. "I guess I'm just not a pet person," she said. She looked at Carla. "Mites! Carla will never win a prize looking like that."

Lisa and Mandy looked at each other. There were tears in Lisa's eyes, but Jennifer didn't notice.

"Are you coming?" she said to her little sister.

"Why don't you stay for a little while, Lisa?" Mrs Hope said. "I'm sure Mandy would like that."

Mandy looked at her mother gratefully. "Gran and Grandad are coming round," she said to Lisa. "Gran is bringing some of the doughnuts she's made."

Lisa tried to smile but it was a real effort for her.

"That would be nice," she said. "Can I stay here with Carla for a little while?"

Mrs Hope nodded. "Of course you can," she said. "I'll show you what we do to get rid of mites."

Jennifer shuddered again. "Rather you

than me," she said. "Don't be late home, Lisa. I'll tell Mum you're staying for a while."

Mandy watched as Jennifer closed the surgery door behind her. "Some people!" she said.

"Now, now, Mandy," Mrs Hope said. "Not everybody is prepared for the work that goes into keeping a pet. At least Jennifer realises she hasn't done very well."

"Hmmph!" said Mandy. Then she looked at Lisa.

Lisa was bending over Carla, stroking her shabby fur, talking to her.

"At least I can talk to her and play with her – until she goes to a new home," Lisa said.

Mrs Hope smiled. "I've got an idea about that," she said.

"Oh, Mum, what?" said Mandy.

Mrs Hope shook her head. "Let's get Carla better first," she said. "That's the most important thing."

Mandy nodded her head. "Of course it is," she agreed.

"Lisa, would you like to help?" Mrs Hope asked. "Or perhaps you don't like mites either."

Lisa picked Carla up and cuddled her. "I *don't* like mites," she replied. "Not when they make Carla scratch all her fur off. But that doesn't mean I won't touch Carla. Of course I want to help."

Mrs Hope smiled. "There you are," she said. "I knew it!"

"What?" asked Mandy.

"Lisa is a born pet lover," Mrs Hope said. "I think we're going to have to think of a very special home for Carla!"

5

A good idea!

"So, how do we get rid of these mites?" Mandy asked.

"We have to bathe the guinea-pig in this," Mrs Hope said, taking a bottle down from a shelf and putting it on the counter.

She ran warm water into a bowl while

Mandy looked at the liquid in the bottle.

"What does that do?" asked Lisa.

"It kills the mites," said Mrs Hope. "If we don't get rid of them Carla could get very sick indeed."

"You mean she might die?" Lisa said.

Mrs Hope nodded. She picked up the bottle and carefully measured a small amount of the liquid into a dish. Then she poured it into the bowl of water.

"Mandy, you get a fresh towel, and Lisa, you hand Carla to me when I ask for her."

Mrs Hope put on a pair of fine rubber gloves, swirled the mixture in the bowl around to mix it thoroughly, and held out her hands for Carla.

Lisa placed the little guinea-pig carefully into Mrs Hope's hands.

"We have to make sure the mixture soaks right down into her skin," explained Mrs Hope. "It won't work otherwise."

"And what then?" asked Lisa.

"Then we wait for a fortnight," said Mrs Hope. "We might have to do this

again. But with any luck one treatment should do the trick."

Mandy and Lisa watched as Mrs Hope scooped the solution over Carla, being careful to cover all her fur. Carla didn't mind at all. She seemed to really like the warm water.

"There," said Mrs Hope at last. "I think that's enough. Ready with that towel, Mandy?"

Mandy spread the fluffy white towel out

on the examination table and Mrs Hope placed Carla in the middle of it.

"Now what?" asked Mandy.

"Lisa, wrap the towel round Carla and let her dry naturally," Mrs Hope said. "And that's it."

"You mean she'll get better now?" said Lisa.

"I hope so," said Mrs Hope.

Mandy watched as Lisa wrapped the little animal up in the soft towel. Mrs Hope was also watching Lisa. Lisa was so gentle with Carla.

"Isn't it awful that Lisa is going to lose Carla?" Mandy said to Mrs Hope. "Couldn't we keep her here until she's better? Then maybe Jennifer would take her back – once Carla looks nice again."

Mrs Hope smiled. "You know the rules, Mandy," she said. "If we kept all the animals you wanted us to keep, we'd have no room for patients!"

Mandy nodded. She knew what her mum said made sense.

Lisa looked up. "At least I can look after her today," she said. "And maybe I can see her before she goes to her new home. Jennifer never let me do this before."

Lisa stood with Carla wrapped up in the towel in her arms. There were tears in her eyes. She really was going to miss Carla.

"What if we sent her to people who would let you come and visit?" Mrs Hope suggested.

"That would be wonderful," Lisa said.

"And what if these people let you try to get Carla back into condition?" said Mrs Hope.

"You mean so that Jennifer would take her back?" said Lisa.

Mrs Hope put her head on one side. "Jennifer has a lot to learn about looking after pets," she said. "Pet's don't win prizes if they aren't well looked after."

"I would *love* to look after Carla," Lisa said.

"*I* would like Jennifer to see what a difference taking care of a pet makes," Mrs Hope said. "And to see that if you want your pet to win a prize, *somebody* has to look after it."

"You mean Lisa," said Mandy.

"I think Lisa would make a wonderful nurse for Carla," Mrs Hope said. "Far better than Jennifer."

"If we can get Carla back into condition then Jennifer might even want to put her into the Show," said Lisa. "But she still won't like looking after her."

"But she might let *you* look after her," said Mandy.

Mrs Hope nodded. "That's what I was thinking," she said. "That way, everybody would be happy. Jennifer would have her prize-winning guinea-pig and Lisa would be able to take care of Carla."

"Oh, that would be wonderful, Mrs Hope," Lisa said eagerly. Then she looked doubtful. "But what about Mum? She's made up her mind that Carla has to go. I don't think she would trust me to look after Carla – not after all that trouble with Jennifer."

Mrs Hope smiled. "Well, *I* think you'd be very good at looking after a pet, Lisa," she said. "But we'd have to prove that to Jennifer – and to your mum."

"It's worth a try," said Mandy.

"But I can't take her home," said Lisa. "So where is she going to live?"

Mrs Hope's eyes twinkled. "Who's coming round?" she said, teasing.

Mandy's mouth dropped open. "Gran and Grandad," she said. "They'll do it. I'm sure they will. Mum, you're brilliant!"

Lisa looked at Mandy and Mrs Hope. "You mean they'll look after Carla for me? They'll let me come and visit?"

"Of course they will," Mandy said. "All we have to do is ask them!"

6

Carla's new home

"A guinea-pig?" Grandad said as they sat round the kitchen table at Animal Ark munching doughnuts. "We've never had a guinea-pig before."

"You'll love Carla," Mandy said. "Lisa and I will take you to visit her in a minute. She's beautiful."

"She doesn't look her best at the moment," Lisa explained. "But usually she does look beautiful."

"I'm sure she does," Gran said, smiling at Lisa. "And we'll be glad to keep her for you for a few weeks."

"There now," Mrs Hope said. "Gran and Grandad to the rescue!"

"We'll come over to Lilac Cottage every day to see Carla," Mandy said.

"We'll clean out her cage and feed her and everything," Lisa promised. "She won't be any trouble, honestly."

"But what are you going to say to Jennifer?" Gran said. "Won't she want to know where Carla has gone?"

"We can tell her the truth," said Mandy. "We can say you and Grandad are looking after Carla. But we don't have to tell her our plan."

"I suppose not," Gran said. "After all, Carla will be well looked after and that's the main thing."

"Exactly," said Mandy.

"You'll have to give us a few lessons in looking after guinea-pigs though," Grandad said.

Lisa nodded. "I've got a book at home. I'll lend it to you."

"When do you think Carla will be ready to go to her new home, Mum?" Mandy asked.

Mrs Hope smiled. "I think she should be ready tomorrow evening," she said. "But I'd like to make sure her treatment is working before I send her off."

"She'll need careful grooming for a few weeks," Mrs Hope added.

"But her coat will grow back, won't it?" asked Lisa.

Mrs Hope nodded. "Of course it will," she said. "It might not be as perfect as it was before, but there's no reason why she shouldn't make a full recovery."

"I'll buy a baby hairbrush," Lisa said. "The Guinea-pig Gang told me that would be good to use for grooming. Oh, it's so wonderful to have the chance to look after Carla."

Lisa's eyes were shining with happiness. "Thanks, Gran," Mandy whispered. "Thanks a lot!"

Lisa jumped up. "Do you want to see Carla now?" she said to Mandy's gran and grandad.

Gran smiled. "Of course!" she said.

Grandad got up from his chair. Lisa was already half-way to the door, eager to show Carla off.

"If she's going to come and live with us, we'll have to introduce ourselves," he said. "Do you think she'll like us?"

Lisa nodded her head as she swung the kitchen door open. "Come and see," she said. "Carla will love you. I just know she will!"

Mandy, Lisa and James stopped off at the post office on the way home from school the next day.

"Mrs McFarlane sells everything," James said as they pushed open the post-office door. "She's bound to have a baby hairbrush."

"A hairbrush!" said a voice. "You certainly look as if you could do with a hairbrush, James Hunter. Your hair is falling into your eyes."

James shoved his hair away from his eyes and his glasses slipped down his nose.

"Hello, Mrs Ponsonby," Mandy said. "How is Pandora?"

Mrs Ponsonby was a large, bossy woman with pink glasses. She was wearing a bright-blue hat with a feather in it and carrying a Pekinese under her arm.

"She's very well," Mrs Ponsonby said, as Mandy tickled the little dog under the chin. "What do you want a hairbrush for?"

It was no use trying to avoid Mrs Ponsonby or her questions. It was easier just to answer them.

"It's for a guinea-pig," Mandy said. "A baby's hairbrush is good for grooming."

"Really?" said Mrs Ponsonby. "I

wonder if I should try that with my Pandora."

"I've got some baby hairbrushes here somewhere," said Mrs McFarlane from behind the counter. "Now where did I see them?"

Mandy grinned. Mrs McFarlane's shop was like an Aladdin's cave. The shelves were full to overflowing with all sorts of things. It was Mandy and James's favourite shop in the village.

"There they are," said James, pointing to a box on the top shelf near the door.

"Now what are they doing up there?" Mrs McFarlane said. "I'll just get the stepladder."

Mrs McFarlane bustled off into the back of the shop.

"Oh, look!" said Lisa. "There's a notice about the Welford Show." She read it eagerly. "There it is – there's the guinea-pig competition," she said.

"So it's *your* guinea-pig you want the hairbrush for," Mrs Ponsonby said to Lisa.

Lisa bit her lip. "Not exactly," she said.

Mrs Ponsonby looked suspicious.

"It's really my sister Jennifer's guinea-pig," Lisa said. "But Mandy's gran and grandad are going to look after it for a little while and I'm going to help them."

Mrs Ponsonby looked puzzled, but Mrs McFarlane came back with the stepladder at that moment and set it up next to the shelves.

"You can fetch down one of those hairbrushes for me too," Mrs Ponsonby said. "That pink one looks nice."

Mrs McFarlane was halfway up the stepladder. "This one?" she said, pointing to a pale-pink one.

Mrs Ponsonby put Pandora down on the floor and pointed again. "No, no," she said. "That nice *bright*-pink one."

Pandora scampered over to the ladder and tried to jump up on the first step.

"Now then, sweetums," Mrs Ponsonby said to the little Pekinese. "Don't be naughty. Come back."

Pandora looked round and barked. She hopped up on the first step of the ladder just as Mrs Ponsonby made a lunge for her.

"Whoops," said Mrs Ponsonby as she missed Pandora and bumped into the ladder. Her hat fell down over her eyes, the feather waving wildly.

"Watch out!" Lisa called as the ladder wobbled.

James made a dive for the ladder and grabbed it. "Hold on," he shouted.

Mrs McFarlane clutched the ladder tightly. Pandora barked and sprang off the step, wrapping her lead round James's ankles. The ladder began to wobble again.

"Help, Mandy!" James called.

Mandy leaped to the ladder and clutched at it. Mrs McFarlane hung on.

"Be careful, James," Mrs Ponsonby shouted. "Mind you don't stand on my poor Pandora."

Pandora wrapped her lead even further

round James's ankles. He looked at Mandy and made a face.

"It's all right, Mrs Ponsonby. I couldn't move even if I wanted to," James said.

Mrs Ponsonby scooped Pandora up. She yanked the lead free of James's legs – he overbalanced and sat down suddenly on the floor.

"Really! You children!" Mrs Ponsonby said, shaking her head. "Poor Pandora is scared out of her wits."

Pandora struggled to get down again but Mrs Ponsonby held on to her. The little peke didn't look in the least bit scared.

"Us?" said James. "It wasn't *our* fault."

Mandy clutched the ladder tightly. "Are you all right, Mrs McFarlane?"

Mrs McFarlane looked down at them. "If you ask me, I think I'm in the safest place," she said. "Now, what about these hairbrushes? What colour do you want, Lisa?"

Lisa was shaking with laughter. "Oh,

pink!" she said. "Make mine pink too."

"I think I'll bring the whole box down," Mrs McFarlane suggested. "It'll be safer."

Mandy, James and Lisa watched as Mrs Ponsonby paid for her hairbrush and magazines and sailed out of the shop.

"She didn't even apologise," Lisa said.

Mandy grinned. "Mrs Ponsonby *never* apologises."

"That's because Mrs Ponsonby is never wrong," Mrs McFarlane added, and winked.

"Come on," said James, dusting himself down. "Let's go and see if Carla is ready to go to her new home!"

Carla *was* ready.

"She seems fine," Mrs Hope said. "She hasn't been scratching at all today. But I'll still need to see her in two weeks' time to make sure."

"So can we take her to Gran and Grandad's?" Mandy asked.

Mrs Hope nodded. "Tell Gran to keep her away from draughts as much as possible. Poor Carla will be a bit cold until her coat grows again."

Mandy and James put Carla's feed and hay in plastic bags and Lisa picked up the cage.

"Ready?" she said to the other two.

"Ready!" said Mandy and James.

"Hi, Gran! Hi, Grandad!" Mandy called as they pushed open the gate at Lilac Cottage. "We've brought your visitor."

Gran and Grandad came to the door and looked at the cage Lisa was holding.

"My, my," Gran said. "She looks better already."

"Do you think so?" Lisa asked, as she and Mandy came up the garden path.

Grandad nodded. "She looks a lot less sorry for herself than she did last night," he said. "She's as bright as a button."

"Come on in and let's get her settled down," said Gran.

Lisa carried Carla into the kitchen.

"I thought we would keep her in the

utility room," Gran said, leading them into a little room off the kitchen. "It's nice and warm in here."

"It's perfect," said Lisa, setting the cage down on the worktop.

"This is great," said Mandy. "Mum and Dad said to keep her out of draughts. She'll be really cosy in here."

"She seems happy enough already," Gran said to Lisa with a smile. "Look! She's made herself right at home."

Lisa looked at Carla. The little guinea-pig settled down on her haunches and began to clean her whiskers.

"Oh, Carla," Lisa said. "I think you're going to like your new home a lot."

"Now," said Grandad. "You'd better give us our first lesson. We've got a lot to learn about guinea-pigs."

Lisa filled Carla's water bottle and fixed it to the bars of her cage.

"She needs lots of fresh water," she said. "Guinea-pigs get thirsty just like us."

"I'm glad you mentioned that," said Grandad. "How about a cup of tea while we've having our lesson?"

"And ginger biscuits?" added Mandy.

"Of course," Gran said.

Mandy smiled. Carla was going to be well looked after. And maybe, soon, she would be back at home with Lisa. Mandy crossed her fingers. Their plan just *had* to work!

7

Bad news

Carla's coat soon began to grow again. Lisa visited Lilac Cottage every day to play with Carla and to groom her. Most days Mandy and James went along too.

Sometimes Pam brought Ginny to play with Carla.

"Oh, look at them," said Lisa one

evening at Gran's. "They're so happy together."

The two guinea-pigs were chasing each other round the back garden. Grandad had made a run for Carla so that she could have some exercise every day.

"Carla's coat is nearly back to normal," Pam said.

Mandy nodded happily. "Mum checked her last week," she said. "The

mites are all gone and Mum thinks Carla is going to make a complete recovery. Her coat is going to be just as beautiful as ever."

"She's certainly a much happier little guinea-pig than when I *first* saw her," Gran said, looking at the two little animals scampering about the grass and tumbling over each other. "It's lovely to see her playing like that. You're quite right, Pam. Guinea-pigs do like company."

"Maybe it's time Carla joined the Guinea-pig Gang," Pam said.

Lisa's eyes lit up. "What a good idea," she said. "I'm sure Carla would love that."

"Why don't you have your next meeting here?" Gran suggested.

"Terrific," said Pam. "I'll let the Gang know. Is it all right if we come this Friday?"

Gran nodded. "I'll make some of my extra-special ginger biscuits," she said.

The Guinea-pig Gang assembled at Lilac Cottage right on time. The only person missing was Lisa. Mandy frowned. It wasn't like Lisa to be late – not when she was coming to visit Carla.

"There's going to be a special section for Pedigree guinea-pigs," Ross was saying. "There are people coming from all over the place to show their guinea-pigs."

Mandy smiled. She was really looking forward to the Welford Show and so were the rest of the Guinea-pig Gang. They were all going to see the guinea-pig competition and cheer Carla on.

"Here comes Lisa," said James.

"Hi!" Mandy called.

Lisa raised her hand and waved, but she looked very worried.

"What's wrong?" asked Mandy.

Lisa bit her lip. "Mum has been talking to Mrs Ponsonby," she said.

"What about?" asked James.

"About Carla," Lisa said. "Mrs Ponsonby told Mum that she had seen me buying a hairbrush for my guinea-pig. So I had to tell Mum all about visiting Carla at Lilac Cottage. I told her Carla was coming on so well Jennifer would want to take her back and put her in for the Show after all."

"That's just like Mrs Ponsonby," James said. "Interfering again!"

"What did your mum say?" asked Mandy.

"She says Jennifer can't have Carla back," Lisa said. "She says it isn't fair to Carla."

"Didn't you tell her you would look after Carla?" Pam asked.

Lisa nodded. "Mum said if Jennifer couldn't look after a guinea-pig then neither can I. She says I'm too young."

"But that isn't true," said Mandy. "You look after Carla beautifully. Why don't you ask your mum to come and see Carla? Then she'll see how well you can look after her."

Lisa shook her head. "She says your gran and grandad are looking after her, not me."

"But *you* taught *us* how to look after her," Gran said.

"It's no good," said Lisa. "Jennifer complained so much about Carla it made Mum change her mind about having a pet."

"That isn't fair," said Pam. "You're brilliant with Carla."

"Thanks," said Lisa. "But there's no point in Jennifer putting Carla in for the Show now."

"What a pity," said Pam. "I'm entering Ginny in the pet guinea-pig competition. In fact the Guinea-pig Gang are all entering their pets. I thought we could all go to the Show together."

Mandy's face lit up. "*I* know!" she said. "Why don't *you* enter Carla in the pedigree section, Lisa? And if she wins a prize, your mum will see how well you've looked after her."

Lisa shook her head. "Mum isn't going to the Show."

"But she's just *got* to see her," said Pam.

"How?" Mandy asked. "We can't drag her round to Lilac Cottage."

"No, but we could take Carla to see *her*," James suggested.

Lisa shrugged. "It wouldn't do any good," she said. "Mum says Carla deserves a home with somebody who is old enough to look after her properly."

Gran appeared at the kitchen door.

"Oh, Gran, did you hear that?" Mandy said anxiously. "Lisa's mum won't have Carla back."

"Hold on," said Gran. "Calm down and start at the beginning. I'm sure things aren't as bad as they seem."

Mandy took a deep breath. Maybe Gran was right. There had to be a way round the problem.

Mandy explained and Gran looked thoughtful. Mandy waited, hardly daring to breathe.

"How many weeks is it till the Show?" Gran asked.

"Two," James replied.

"Well," Gran said slowly, "that isn't very long. I'll have to get a move on if I'm going to get all that baking done in time. And I'll need some help with the stall."

Mandy looked at her gran in puzzlement. Her heart sank. Baking! What about Carla? Surely Gran wasn't more interested in her stall at the Show?

Gran smiled at Lisa. "Do you think your mum would help me with my stall if I asked her?"

"Of course she would," Lisa said.

"So she *would* be at the Show after all," James said, catching on to Gran's meaning.

Mandy let her breath out. "And then you could make sure she saw Carla. Gran, you're so clever!"

Lisa still looked a little doubtful.

"It'll work," said James reassuringly.

"*If* Carla wins a prize," Lisa said. "Oh, I hope she does."

"She will," said Mandy. "Of course she will!"

8

The Welford Show

Gran and Grandad had already arrived at the Welford Show when Mandy and James got there. Mandy looked around the church field where the Show took place every year.

There were tents set up here and there for the stalls. There was a tombola and a coconut shy and even a greased pole. Mandy saw Peter Foster trying to climb it. He was nearly at the top. Timmy was scampering round the bottom of the pole, barking his head off.

The field was crowded with people – the whole of Welford seemed to be there. This was going to be the best Show ever!

"He's nearly made it," said James, watching Peter.

As they watched, Peter reached for the top – and his hand slipped. He came sliding all the way down to the bottom. Timmy started to leap up at him while Peter tried to fend him off.

"Peter looks as if he needs a bath," said Mr Hope, laughing.

"And so does Timmy – now!" Mandy said.

"There's Gran's stall," Mrs Hope said, pointing to a tent at the edge of the field. "Why don't you go and say hello, Mandy?"

Mandy was looking around, her eyes glowing with excitement. She could see Laura Baker with her rabbits; Fluffy, Nibbles and Patch. Richard Tanner had Duchess safely in her cat basket and Gary had Gertie draped round his neck.

"Look at all the pets," she said. "Isn't it wonderful?"

Mr and Mrs Hope laughed. "There are enough here to satisfy even you, Mandy," Mr Hope said.

"Come on," James said to Mandy. "Let's go and ask your gran where Lisa and Carla are. I can't see them, can you?"

Mandy dragged her eyes away from a cage with two adorable black-and-white kittens in it.

"Lisa was coming with her mum and Jennifer," Mandy said. "Gran and Grandad were bringing Carla."

Mandy and James made their way to Gran's stall. Mrs Glover was arranging cakes on a plate and Gran was unpacking more goodies from plastic boxes.

"Hi, Gran. Hi, Mrs Glover," Mandy said.

"Hello, you two," Mrs Glover said. "Are you entering Blackie in one of the competitions, James?"

James looked at Blackie and shook his head. "Not this year," he said. "Blackie is a bit young yet."

"Next year, then," Mrs Glover said. "Blackie is such a lovely puppy. He looks like a prize-winner to me."

James looked thoughtful. "Maybe," he said. "But only the very best pets win prizes."

"That's right," Mandy said quickly. "A pet has got to be really special to win."

"*And* well looked after," Mrs Glover said. "Keeping a pet is a big responsibility."

"But if you really love animals then you *like* looking after them," Mandy said.

Mrs Glover looked thoughtful. "I suppose you do," she said. "Lisa is very fond of animals but she's too young to have a pet."

"Lisa is the same age as me," James pointed out.

"Is she?" said Mrs Glover, looking even more thoughtful. "Your Gran has been telling me how good Lisa is with Carla, Mandy."

"Oh, she is," said Mandy. "You'd be surprised, Mrs Glover."

Out of the corner of her eye, Mandy saw Gran wink at her.

"Lisa is looking for you," said Gran. "I think she has something to show you."

"Where is she?" James asked.

Gran nodded towards a group of children gathered in a corner of the field.

"The Guinea-pig Gang," Mandy said. "See you later, Gran. Bye, Mrs Glover."

Mandy and James made their way towards the Guinea-pig Gang. Lisa was right in the middle of it – with Carla.

Mandy put a finger through the bars of Carla's cage and the little animal sniffed delicately at it.

"She's looking great," Mandy said. "Her coat is just as nice as ever."

"Does your mum know Carla is here?" James asked Lisa.

Lisa shook her head. Her eyes were bright with excitement. "Mandy's grandad smuggled her in," she said. "I thought I would keep her out of Mum's way until the competition."

"Good thinking," Mandy said. "After

all, we don't want to spoil the surprise, do we?"

Lisa smiled nervously. "I hope it works," she said, looking at Carla.

James smiled. "Mandy's gran has been telling your mum how good you are at looking after Carla," he said.

"I think your mum might be starting to change her mind already," said Mandy. "Just wait till she sees Carla."

"We'd still have to persuade Jennifer to take Carla back," Lisa said.

"Oh, that won't be a problem," Mandy said. "Not once Carla has won a prize!"

"And now for the pedigree guinea-pig competition," the announcer said. "Would all the owners please bring their guinea-pigs forward to the judges' table?"

Lisa looked at Mandy and James. "Wish me luck," she said.

Mandy gave her a thumbs-up sign but James was looking round.

"Where's Jennifer?" he asked.

Mandy looked around too. Gran was walking towards them with Mrs Glover at her side. Mrs Glover looked slightly puzzled. But there was no sign of Jennifer.

"We'll find her," Mandy said. "Good luck, Lisa!"

Mandy and James watched Lisa move forward with Carla in her cage. There were five other pure-bred guinea-pigs in the competition – a black-and-white Dutch, two rosetted Abyssinians, a self golden and a beautiful white Himalayan with brown-grey markings. Carla was up against very stiff competition indeed.

"Come on," urged James. "We don't have much time."

Mandy raced after him, in and out of the crowd, searching furiously. Jennifer was nowhere to be seen.

"She must be around somewhere," said Mandy.

"There she is," James said, pointing to a group of girls in the corner.

"Jennifer!" Mandy called.

Jennifer looked round and frowned. "What is it?" she asked, coming over to them.

"We want to show you something," James said.

"What?" said Jennifer.

"Just come with us – please, Jennifer," Mandy pleaded.

Jennifer shrugged her shoulders. "All right then, but it had better be worth it."

Mandy and James almost dragged her over to the pedigree guinea-pig competition.

"I'm not interested in guinea-pigs any more," Jennifer said, when she saw where they were going.

"But you *will* be," said James. "Wait and see."

Mandy made her way through the crowds to the front of the judges' table. The chief judge was just taking Carla out of her cage.

"Look," Mandy said. "It's Carla."

Jennifer's mouth dropped open. "Carla!" she said. "It can't be. Her coat was a mess."

"It isn't any longer," James said. "Lisa has been looking after her."

"Lisa?" said Jennifer.

"Shh," Mandy said. "They're going to announce the winner."

Mandy hardly dared to breathe as the chief judge stood up. Lisa was standing in front of Carla's cage, her eyes round with excitement.

"We've got an exceptionally fine

collection of guinea-pigs here," the judge said. "But there can only be one winner." He paused and Mandy swallowed hard.

"Carla," James whispered.

"Abby, the Abyssinian," the judge said.

"Oh, no," Mandy said. "Poor Lisa!"

Lisa was still standing in front of the judges' table. She bit her lip, holding back the tears. Then, as the judge awarded the rosette to the Abyssinian guinea-pig, Lisa picked up Carla's cage, turned away and walked towards them.

Mandy tried to smile but it was impossible. Then she saw her gran and Mrs Glover making their way through the crowd towards them.

"It's all right, Lisa," James said, as Lisa came up. "You did your best and so did Carla."

Lisa looked miserably at them both. Then she looked at Jennifer.

"I didn't know you were entering Carla for this competition," Jennifer said.

Lisa looked down at Carla. "I'm sorry,

Jennifer," she said. "I suppose I should have asked you, but I didn't think you'd let me do it."

"I wouldn't have," Jennifer said, staring at Carla. "I can't believe my eyes. Look at Carla's coat!"

A tall man, one of the judges, passed by and heard her.

"Make sure you enter Carla next year," he said to Lisa. He looked at the others. "Lisa told me about the mites," he went on. "I'm afraid Carla's coat hasn't quite recovered. If it had, she would certainly have won. I've never seen such a fine Tort and White. Somebody has obviously taken very good care of her." He smiled at Lisa and walked on.

"Well," Mrs Glover said to Lisa. "I certainly *am* surprised. Mandy's gran told me you had taken good care of Carla, but I didn't realise just how well you had looked after her, Lisa."

Lisa tried to smile as she handed Carla's cage to Gran. "I wonder if you would mind keeping her until we find a proper home for her," she said.

"You can't give her away now," said Jennifer.

Lisa spun round in surprise. "Well, *you* don't want her. That's why I entered her in the competition. I thought you might want to take her back if she won a prize."

"Is *that* why you did all this?" Jennifer asked softly.

Lisa nodded, hardly able to speak. "I thought she could win prizes for you and I could do all the work of looking after her. I love looking after her."

Jennifer looked at her mother. "Oh, Mum," she said. "We can't let Carla go – not now. I'm sorry I didn't take care of her properly. Lisa was right all along. I should have let her share Carla."

"Are you saying you would look after Carla now?" Mrs Glover asked.

Jennifer shook her head. "Not me," she said. "You were right. Pets need people who *really* love them. I'm not a pet person."

"But *I* am," said Lisa eagerly. "Oh, Mum, can I take care of Carla? I promise I'll look after her — honestly."

Mrs Glover looked from Jennifer to Lisa. "I don't know—" she began.

"Lisa *can* look after Carla, Mum," Jennifer said. "She's proved it. And she's taught me a lesson."

"I'm certainly glad you've learned your lesson about pets, Jennifer," Mrs Glover said.

Gran gave a little cough and Mrs Glover looked at her. "What do you think, Dorothy?"

Gran smiled. "I don't think Carla could have a better owner than Lisa," she said.

"I agree," Jennifer said. "Lisa *deserves* to have Carla for her pet."

Mrs Glover looked at Lisa and Carla. "It's your birthday soon, Lisa," she said.

Lisa looked puzzled. "Yes," she said. "In two weeks."

"I think Jennifer is right," Mrs Glover said, smiling. "I'll tell you what. Jennifer

can have a personal stereo after all, and Lisa, you can have Carla for your birthday. How's that?"

"Brilliant!" said Jennifer.

"Perfect!" Lisa said, then turned to Mandy and James. "Did you hear that? I can have Carla for my very own."

Just then Pam Stanton came rushing up. "Guess what?" she said. "Ginny won the pet guinea-pig competition. The Guinea-pig Gang are going to celebrate, and you and Carla are invited, Lisa."

Pam rushed off again and Lisa watched her go. "You know," she said, "I don't care if Carla *never* wins a prize – just so long as she's *my* guinea-pig."

Mandy and James smiled at her.

"Do you think we're invited to the Guinea-pig Gang's celebration as well?" James asked.

"Of course you are," Lisa said. "You're honorary members."

"And you're a *proper* member now," said Mandy.

Lisa grinned. "Did you hear that, Carla?" she said. "We're fully-fledged members of the Guinea-pig Gang – both of us!"

LUCY DANIELS

Animal Ark™

Gerbil
Genius

Hodder
Children's
Books

A division of Hachette Children's Books

Special thanks to Pat Posner

Text copyright © 1998 Working Partners Ltd.
Created by Working Partners Limited, London W6 0QT
Original series created by Ben M. Baglio
Illustrations copyright © 1998 Paul Howard

First published as a single volume in Great Britain in 1998
by Hodder Children's Books

Contents

1

Mouse-counting day

Mandy Hope was standing at her bedroom window listening to the church bells ringing out over Welford village. Her grandad was one of the bell-ringers and Mandy sometimes tried to guess which bell he was ringing.

But today, Mandy was waiting

impatiently for the bells to stop. Then she could go and meet Grandad, and her best friend James Hunter and his dad, who lived at the other end of the village. The four of them had something very special to do this morning.

Mandy stuck her head further out of the window. The sun was shining but there was a gentle breeze and she smiled as it ruffled her hair. Perfect weather.

Suddenly Mandy heard another sound – a fretful whining coming from the modern building attached to the back of the cottage. Mandy's parents were both vets at Animal Ark, and the extension was their surgery. The whining was coming from the unit, a special room where animals stayed if they weren't quite well enough to go home.

That will be Sasha, Mandy told herself, drawing her head back inside. She decided to ask her mum if she could give the dog a quick cuddle.

Mrs Hope was just on her way through

to the surgery when Mandy bounded downstairs. "Can I go and see Sasha, Mum?" asked Mandy, as her mum opened the door that led from the house to the surgery.

"OK. Just for a minute or two," Mrs Hope replied.

Sasha was an Afghan hound. She'd had a small lump removed from her eyelid. "She'll be going home today," said Emily Hope. She smiled as she watched Mandy stroking the beautiful dog.

"What about Smudge?" asked Mandy, moving to another large cage where a young black-and-white cat was pacing restlessly up and down. Smudge had been in a fight with another cat and he'd had to have stitches in his ear.

"Yes. He can go home too," said Mrs Hope. "I'll phone Naomi Bruce in a little while and tell her she can come and fetch him."

"That's good," said Mandy. "He doesn't like being shut up in this cage, do you,

boy?" Mandy rubbed his nose through the bars. Smudge glared at her and miaowed loudly.

"Come on," said Mrs Hope. "We'll leave them to settle now."

They went through into the cottage and Mandy hurried into the kitchen and ran to the back door. "The bells have stopped," she said. "I can go and meet Grandad now!"

"Why? Are you going somewhere with him?" asked Mr Hope, as he came into the kitchen.

"Dad! You haven't *really* forgotten what's happening today, have you?" said Mandy.

"Stop teasing her, Adam." Mrs Hope laughed. "You know why Mandy's meeting Grandad."

"And James and his dad," Mandy added happily.

Mr Hope smiled and pointed to the calendar on the kitchen wall. Next to today's date, Mandy had written the words "MOUSE-COUNTING DAY" in big red letters. "I could hardly forget what you're doing today, could I?" he chuckled. "Off you go then, and good luck."

"Don't forget to take the mixed seed," said Emily Hope, pointing to two brown paper bags on the kitchen table.

"Thanks, Mum." Mandy picked them up. "I'll see you both later," she said and hurried off.

The others were waiting for her outside the post office.

"We thought you were never coming, Mandy," said James when she raced up to them. "Dad and I have been here for ages."

"I went into the unit to see Sasha and Smudge," puffed Mandy as she hugged Grandad. "It must have taken longer than I thought."

Mr Hunter smiled. "Don't take any notice of James, Mandy. We've only been here a couple of minutes. We arrived at the same time as your grandad."

"Well, it seemed like ages to me," said James, shoving his glasses further on to the bridge of his nose.

They turned on to the narrow lane at the side of the post office. This was a short-cut to the river. As they hurried along, they saw Mrs Ponsonby walking towards them. She lived in Bleakfell Hall; a huge grey-stone house on the outskirts of Welford. But she often came down into the village – she liked to keep an eye on what was happening there.

Mrs Ponsonby was wearing a large straw hat with poppies around the brim and a white dress with a pattern of blue, red, yellow and orange flowers all over it.

"She looks like a flower shop," James whispered to Mandy.

Mandy nodded and smiled. Mrs Ponsonby always seemed to wear colourful clothes and big hats. Then Mandy noticed Pandora, Mrs Ponsonby's plump Pekinese. Pandora was tucked under Mrs Ponsonby's arm as usual and *she* was wearing a straw hat, too!

"The poor little darling gets so hot," said Mrs Ponsonby when she saw Mandy looking at the hat. "She begged so hard to go for a walk along the riverbank – I put her sunhat on so she wouldn't get sunstroke.

"Good morning, Mr Hope, Mr Hunter," she added as Grandad and James's dad got close. "You'll never guess what someone has done to the reedbeds!"

Mrs Ponsonby didn't wait for a reply. She continued indignantly, "Someone has

dumped lots of old tennis balls there. It's
a disgrace, that's what it is. I'm going to
report it to the parish council first thing
tomorrow and have them removed."

Mandy and James gazed at each other
in dismay. Then Mandy blurted out,
"You didn't *do* anything to the tennis
balls, did you, Mrs Ponsonby? You see,
we put them there. I mean, some of us
from school put them there."

"They're special feeding houses," added
James. "The balls have got little holes in
one side for a door and we slotted a
bamboo cane through two slits on the
back of each ball."

"Then we stuck the canes upright into
the ground and put some mixed seed inside
each mouse house," said Mandy. "And—'

"*Mouse* house?" interrupted Mrs
Ponsonby.

Mandy nearly giggled. She thought Mrs
Ponsonby had sounded a bit like a mouse
herself just then.

Then Grandad explained that Mandy

and James's school was taking part in a survey to try to find out how common harvest mice were in different areas all over the country.

"In some parts of the country, farmers grow more than one crop of hay or wheat a year," said James. "That means they're cutting the hay and wheat down just at the time the harvest mice want to build their nests. So the survey's to help us find out if they've found different places to live."

"We put fifty mouse houses in the reed-beds on Friday," said Mandy. "Today we're going to check how many have been used. It's our very first mouse-counting day!"

"You mean you're going to look inside each house and see if there's a mouse there?" Mrs Ponsonby shuddered.

Mandy shook her head. "We're going to look inside and see if the seeds we put there have been eaten," she explained. "If they have, it will mean a harvest mouse has eaten them, because the little hole is too small for other creatures to use. Then we'll *know* there are harvest mice here. It will be brilliant if we do find a mouse in a house," she added. "But I don't think we will."

"I still think the tennis balls are a bit of an eyesore," said Mrs Ponsonby. "But," she added, giving a small bow, "seeing as you're carrying out a survey, I won't ask to get them removed."

"Phew!" James breathed out slowly as they watched Mrs Ponsonby totter away on her high-heeled sandals. "Good job we explained things. It would have been awful if she'd done something to get our mouse houses taken away."

"Well, it's sorted now," said Grandad. "So let's get a move on and do something ourselves," he added, smiling down at his granddaughter.

A little while later, Mandy and James had worked their way along one row of mouse houses. Grandad and Mr Hunter were working their way along another row. "Eight of the houses along this row are empty," she said, beaming. "Which means something's eaten the seed, doesn't it, James?"

James nodded happily. "It certainly does!" he said, popping some more seed through a small hole in one of the empty houses.

Mr Hunter told them they'd found five empty houses on their row.

"That means . . ." Mandy did a quick count, ". . . thirteen out of twenty-two mouse houses have been used."

"But," James worked a sum out in his head, "there are still twenty-eight mouse houses to check!"

"How is anyone going to work out how many harvest mice are here?" asked Mr Hunter. "It might just be one eating all the seed."

"It would end up a jolly *big* one, Dad!" said James. Then he added, "Our teachers,

Mrs Black and Mrs Todd, said we won't be able to work *that* out properly."

Mandy nodded. "They said that part of it will have to be guesswork. They said we should count three empty houses as one harvest mouse."

"But the main thing," James said, "is that we know for sure that there *are* harvest mice here."

"Come on then, let's start on the next row!" Mandy hurried over and bent down in front of a mouse house. The cane was quite tall but the tennis-ball house was only about half a metre from the ground.

Mandy carefully pulled the little house off its bamboo cane. She held it in one hand and shook it over the palm of her other. "No seed left in this one!" she said to James.

She replaced the tennis ball and walked a few steps to get some seed. The houses were about a metre apart. She and James were sharing one bag of seed and Grandad and Mr Hunter were sharing the other. "We'll have to tell the others to bring a small bag of seed *each*," Mandy said. "It won't take as long then."

"Good idea," agreed James. "I don't need any for this house, though, as there's still lots of seed in it." He put the house back and walked on, leaving the next one he passed for Mandy to check.

Suddenly Grandad appeared behind the mouse house Mandy was about to check. "I'm sure I heard a noise coming from inside this one," he whispered, bending down.

"You mean there's a mouse inside. Mandy asked excitedly.

Grandad nodded. "I think there could be!" he said.

2

A big surprise

Mandy knelt down to listen and her eyes
widened as she heard a strange little
thumping noise. It lasted for only a second
but she *knew* she'd heard it. Maybe a
harvest mouse was building a nest inside
the feeding house. Mrs Todd, her teacher,
had said that might happen, because the

tennis balls were almost the same size and shape as a harvest mouse's nest.

Mandy signalled urgently to James, then shuffled along on her knees, edging herself closer to the mouse house. She was trying really hard to move silently but the tops of her trainers brushed some reeds and they rustled slightly. Mandy froze and glanced at James as the thumping noise from inside the mouse house started again.

"Wow!" said James, his eyes shining with excitement.

"If that's a harvest mouse, it must be wearing clogs to make that sort of noise!" said Grandad.

James and Mandy listened to the drumming noise and stared at the tennis-ball mouse house. Then James pointed to the door hole. "See that, Mandy? The hole's been made bigger."

"The mouse probably made it bigger so it could carry nesting material in," Mandy whispered. "Maybe it's planning to cover the hole with leaves and grass from the inside. Oh, I wish we could peep in, but that might frighten it and make it run off."

"Let's just watch for a while," James suggested. "It might come out if it thinks we've gone. Then it would be safe to look in."

Mandy nodded. She hoped the harvest mouse *would* come out. She'd never seen a real live one close up. She'd never seen a harvest mouse's nest, either, apart from in photos or on the television. Now she and James might see both. It would be great telling everyone at school about it tomorrow!

Grandad and Mr Hunter finished off the mouse-house count on their own while James and Mandy sat with their eyes glued to the door hole of the tennis ball.

They returned after a while, and crouched down beside Mandy and James.

Grandad said quietly, "We've added all the figures up and, altogether, twenty-eight houses are being used."

"Over half. That's brilliant!" Mandy exclaimed.

"I've written it down in the notebook for you, James," Mr Hunter told him.

"Thanks, Dad," murmured James. "I think Mandy and I will stay on a while, if that's OK?"

"We want to know if the harvest mouse is nesting in there," said Mandy. "We'll come home as soon as we find out."

Another half-hour went by before anything happened. Then a face appeared at the door hole. It was a dark golden colour and, for a moment, two big, round, dark eyes stared unblinkingly at Mandy and James. The creature's ears were standing straight up, and its brown nose and long whiskers were twitching. Then the face disappeared.

Startled, Mandy and James gazed at each other. They'd only seen the creature for a second or two, but they both knew it definitely *wasn't* a harvest mouse!

"It's a gerbil!" Mandy whispered. "Oh, James, the poor little thing must have got out of its cage and made its way outside. Gerbils can't survive out of doors in this country, can they? We'll have to take it to Animal Ark."

James nodded. "But we'd better not try and get it out," he whispered back. "It might escape again. We'll have to carry it there in the mouse house, Mandy."

They got quietly to their feet and tiptoed closer to the tennis ball. They heard the gerbil give a frightened squeak, then saw its face at the door hole again. As quick as a flash, James darted forward and put both hands round the tennis ball, covering the door hole with the palm of one hand.

"Well done," said Mandy with a relieved smile. "It would have been awful if it had got away!"

Keeping the ball clasped firmly between his hands, James straightened up and eased the ball off the cane. "Let's go," he said with a triumphant smile.

As they hurried off to Animal Ark, Mandy couldn't help wondering about the gerbil they had found. They'd got two pet ones in her class at school and Mrs Todd had told them that gerbils burrowed. Mandy wondered why this gerbil had gone into the mouse house rather than tunnelling and making itself a burrow.

"Maybe the soil was too hard or too crumbly for him to dig a burrow," she said aloud.

James nodded and glanced at the ball he was holding tightly in both hands. "I've been thinking about that," he said. "Maybe he did make a burrow some- where. Maybe he came out and saw the harvest mice going into the houses and guessed there was food inside."

"He must have been really hungry," said Mandy. "Or . . ." She clapped her hand over her mouth.

"Or what?" James asked urgently.

"Maybe he's sick or hurt and went in the house to hide because he wasn't *strong* enough to make a burrow!" she said.

There wasn't far to go now. They were both worried by the thought that the gerbil might need help, so they walked as fast as they could.

3

A worrying time

Mrs Hope was sitting in a deckchair on the patio, reading the Sunday paper, when Mandy and James arrived at Animal Ark. Mandy flung open the back gate and dashed across the lawn, leaving James to follow more slowly with the gerbil.

"Mum!" said Mandy, bounding up on to the patio.

Mrs Hope lowered her newspaper. "Is something the matter?" she asked, seeing Mandy's anxious expression.

Mandy nodded and pointed to James who was walking towards them with the mouse house clasped firmly between his hands.

"Grandad said you'd heard noises from inside one of the mouse houses," said Mrs Hope, getting to her feet. "Is it an injured harvest mouse?"

"It's a gerbil, Mrs Hope," said James, looking up with a worried expression.

Emily Hope glanced doubtfully at the mouse house.

"We *both* saw his face, Mum," said Mandy. "We're really sure it's a gerbil."

"OK. We'll go and have a look," said Mrs Hope.

"Oh no!" said Mr Hope as they trooped through the kitchen. "I was just about to make some milkshakes. But something tells me this is another animal rescue."

"Could be," Mrs Hope replied. "Mandy and James think there's a gerbil in this mouse house."

As the three of them went through into the surgery, Mrs Hope asked Mandy to fetch a cardboard pet carrier.

James followed Mrs Hope into the treatment room. She put on her white vet's coat, then smiled at James as he rested his cupped hands on the examination table. "I bet your fingers are aching," she said.

James nodded. "I've been keeping them tightly over the door hole in case the gerbil jumps out and gets away," he said. "We heard him squeaking before but he didn't make any noise all the way here. Do you think he might be sick, Mrs Hope?"

"We'll soon find out, James," Mrs Hope replied, as she pulled on a pair of rubber gloves.

Mandy came in with the pet carrier and put it on the table with a puzzled look.

She couldn't think why her mum wanted such a large box for a gerbil.

When Mrs Hope opened up the carrier she put an empty metal instrument tray in and told James to lower the mouse house to the bottom of the carrier. Then she put her hand over James's. "OK," she said quietly, "move yours away now, James."

James slowly moved his hand from under Mrs Hope's. Then he sighed with relief and wriggled his fingers. But he didn't take his eyes off the mouse house.

"What are you going to do, Mum?" asked Mandy.

"I'm going to tip him into a corner and use the tray as a barrier," her mother explained. "Just in case whatever it is tries to jump."

Mandy and James held their breath as Mrs Hope lifted the tennis ball ever so slightly, tilting it so the door hole was facing towards one corner of the carrier.

A small, browny-gold animal slid out, head first. It quickly rose up on its hind legs, curling its smaller front legs and little clawed feet inwards under its neck, showing the paler colour of its chest and tummy. Although it was the same shape as a mouse, it was a bit bigger.

"Well, it *is* a gerbil!" said Mrs Hope. "I really thought you two had made a mistake, you know," she admitted. "I was expecting a giant harvest mouse to pop out of the mouse house."

For a second the gerbil seemed to be frozen to the spot. Mandy bit her lip. The poor little thing was so scared – its dark chocolate-brown eyes were huge with fright.

Mrs Hope put the ball down gently, then very slowly lifted up one long side of the metal tray, to make it slope. The gerbil lowered its front legs, then, with small, alarmed squeaks, it darted into the corner. It pressed its pointed snout right against the cardboard.

They could see its body trembling and its tail – which was about the same length

as its body – lay straight out behind it, resting on the bottom of the carrier.

The lower half of the gerbil's tail looked really strange. It was as if the fur had been shaved off. It was pink and sore-looking, too! Mandy pointed and lifted worried eyes to her mum's face.

Mrs Hope nodded, straightened up and closed the carrier. "The skin covering his tail has been shed," she explained. "That *can* happen if gerbils are picked up by the end of their tails. In this case, a cat might have clawed at his tail and damaged it."

"Poor gerbil." Mandy sighed. "What happens next, Mum?"

"Well, first I'll put the little chap into a cage and leave him to calm down for a while," she replied.

"Will you be able to make his tail better, Mrs Hope?" asked James.

Emily Hope looked from one worried face to the other. "I'm afraid I'll have to remove most of it," she said gently. "The skin won't grow back. If we leave it like that, the sore part would become infected and make him ill."

Mandy blinked hard. James took off his glasses and wiped them on his T-shirt.

"He should be OK afterwards," Mrs Hope continued. "He just won't be able to balance so well when he's sitting up or jumping."

"But do you really think he'll be OK, Mum?"

"I'll need to take a closer look at him, Mandy. But from what I have seen he appears to be healthy enough. His coat is sleek and in good condition, and there aren't any sore spots round his eyes, ears or nose. He's either not been living wild for long, or he's managed to find the right sort of food to keep him healthy."

"His coat is sleek, isn't it?" said Mandy, looking a bit happier.

"And his eyes are very bright," said James. "But that might be because he's still frightened."

Mrs Hope nodded. She explained that gerbils were often nervous of being handled by someone they didn't know.

"Or," Mandy said thoughtfully, "if he's been living wild for a while, he could have forgotten about humans being friends."

"Yes, that's possible," Mrs Hope agreed. "Now," she added, picking up the carrier, "I'll go and find him a cage and leave him in the unit for a while."

Mandy and James went back through into the kitchen and Mandy told her dad all about the gerbil.

"I wonder where he escaped from," said Mr Hope. "I haven't heard anything about a lost gerbil."

"We need a name for him," said James. "Shall we take Blackie for a walk later and try to think of one?"

"That's an excellent idea, James," said Mr Hope, smiling down at Mandy's friend.

Mandy managed a smile, too. She was still a bit worried about the gerbil but it would be great fun thinking up a name for him. And it would be good to take Blackie for a walk. Blackie was James's Labrador puppy. He hadn't quite learned to do as he was told yet, but Mandy still really loved Blackie.

"I'll call for you right after lunch," said Mandy. "We could drop in at Lilac Cottage afterwards and tell Gran and Grandad about the gerbil."

"Lunch!" James gasped in dismay. "I'm going to be really late. I'd better get going."

Mandy saw James off, then went into the kitchen to get ready for lunch. She kept glancing towards the door, though. She was desperate for her mum to tell her more about the gerbil.

4

Name problems

"He's probably about five or six months old," said Mrs Hope when she came into the kitchen. "I picked him up to put him in the cage and his weight is fine. Apart from his tail, there doesn't seem to be anything wrong with him."

"It's a shame about his tail," Mandy

sighed. "I hope he knows you'll only be doing it to help him."

Mrs Hope gave her a quick hug. "I had a little chat with him and explained what I was going to do and why I had to do it," she replied. "He squeaked at me and I think he was telling me 'OK, I understand'."

Mandy giggled. Her mum knew just how to cheer her up.

While she was eating her lunch, Mandy's mind buzzed with possible names for the gerbil. Sandy . . . Goldie . . . Woffles . . . No! That sounded like a name for a rabbit. Jimmy . . . Jolly . . . Lucky . . . Squeaker . . .

She shook her head. None of them sounded quite right. She'd have to wait and see if James had any better ideas.

When Mandy got close to James's house she could see Blackie's nose poking out through the bars in the front gate. She laughed out loud and Blackie gave a joyful woof. Then he leaped up at the gate, scrabbling his front paws crazily along the top of it.

"He's been looking out for you," said James, dashing forward to get hold of Blackie's collar. "I told him we'd be going for a walk when you got here. I'm sure he understood."

"Of course he did," said Mandy, opening the gate and slipping through. "He's a clever boy. Aren't you, Blackie?"

Blackie's tail wagged furiously and he lowered his head to Mandy's feet. "No, Blackie." Mandy chuckled. "There aren't any laces for you to pull at!"

The Labrador loved pulling at shoe laces, but this afternoon Mandy was wearing flip-flops. Blackie soon found something else to do. He started sniffing and licking at Mandy's bare toes. "Ooh!" She laughed. "That tickles. Stop it, Blackie!"

James pulled Blackie away and clipped his lead on. "Now calm down and walk nicely," he said sternly, opening the gate.

As they walked towards the park, Mandy told her friend what her mum had said. Then she sighed and added, "I expect she'll be seeing to his tail tomorrow, after he's settled a bit."

"It's a pity about his tail," said James. "But it's lucky we found him before it got any worse."

"Lucky's one of the names I thought of while I was eating my lunch," said Mandy.

James wrinkled his nose and shook his head. He didn't think it sounded right, either. They walked on in silence for a while, both trying to think of a good name. But by the time they reached the park, neither of them had thought of one.

"There's Arnie," said Mandy, "sitting next to the bench by the tennis courts."

"Guarding Mr Jordan's bag while he plays tennis," said James.

Mike Jordan was about Grandad Hope's age. He hadn't lived long in Welford but, because of Arnie, he'd soon got to know people.

Everyone loved Arnie. He was a comical-looking dog who was always getting into places he couldn't get himself out of. He was dark brown, tan and white – a cross between a dachshund and a Boston terrier. His body was long and he had a very broad, muscular chest. His front legs curved outwards slightly. They seemed too long for his body, and his tail was long and curled over. He had a really cute face and big ears that stood straight up.

"We'll have to tell Arnie how we rescued the gerbil," James joked as they wandered over to him.

Mandy smiled. Arnie was *always* rescuing things: hedgehogs, baby birds, kittens. If any small creature was where Arnie thought it shouldn't be, he'd pick it up gently in his mouth and take it home. Then, of course, Mr Jordan would have to try to find out where the animal had come from.

"Arnie's name really suits him," Mandy said as she bent down to stroke him. "I wish we could think of a good name for our gerbil."

"*Our* gerbil?" asked James, smiling as Blackie and Arnie greeted each other.

"Well, he's ours for the time being," said Mandy, waving to Mr Jordan as he came to pick up a tennis ball from the back of the court. She knew that if nobody claimed the gerbil they'd have to find him a good home. Her mum and dad were too busy looking after other people's animals for them to have a pet of their own.

"I'm going to ask Mum and Dad if we can look after him," said Mandy. "It would be great, because gerbils are awake in the day. I want to do *everything* for him: feed him, clean his cage, play with him . . ." She paused and nibbled her lip. "He'll have to get used to us before we can play with him. We'll have to talk to him a lot so that he'll come to us when we call him."

"Yup." James frowned. "So he really does need a name. Let's start walking again, Mandy. I can think better then."

They said goodbye to Arnie. He didn't seem to mind them going, and he soon went back to guarding his master's bag.

Mandy noticed a small crowd standing and sitting around the bandstand. "There must be a brass band concert today," she said.

James nodded. "The local band plays here most Sundays. We can hear it from our garden."

"I wonder if Pam Stanton's here, then," said Mandy. "Her dad plays the trombone."

Pam was in Mandy's class at school. She had a guinea-pig called Ginny, and Mandy and James were sure she'd want to hear about the gerbil.

"She is." James pointed. "Look, Mandy. She's over there."

"So are Gran and Grandad!" said Mandy, starting to run.

"Hiya," said Pam, when they dashed up. "Did you manage to see the harvest mouse? Your grandad's just been telling me that you heard one inside a mouse house." She bent down to stroke Blackie.

Mandy and James told Pam, Gran and Grandad about the gerbil.

"Good heavens," said Gran, shaking her head. "Who would have thought it? That's one very clever gerbil."

"It's fantastic!" said Pam. "I wish I'd been there. You'll have to pin a notice on the school bulletin board tomorrow telling everyone you've found a gerbil.

Just think," she continued, "if it hadn't been for our harvest mouse survey—"

"That's it!" James interrupted. "Mandy, I've just thought of a brilliant name for him."

5

Harvey

"Harvey!" James said, beaming triumphantly. "Because we found him in a harvest mouse's house!"

"Harvey," repeated Mandy. "Yes! It's absolutely perfect!"

Pam looked at them and burst out laughing.

"What's up? Don't you like it?" asked Mandy, feeling disappointed.

"It's not that! It's just that . . ." Pam laughed again. ". . . Whenever Dad sees Ginny he wiggles his nose at her, and Mum says he looks more like a *gerbil* than a guinea-pig." She giggled, glancing towards the bandstand where the band members were busy setting everything up. "And Dad's name is Harvey!"

Mandy and James looked towards Mr Stanton. He was holding his trombone to his mouth and Mandy giggled. "Wouldn't our Harvey look funny playing a trombone?" she said.

Gran laughed, too, then she held a finger to her mouth. The concert was about to begin.

The music was soft and slow at first, but gradually it got louder and faster. Blackie sat down. His ears pricked up. He held his head first to one side then to the other, then . . . he pointed his head to the sky and started howling!

"Oh, no!" said James, frantically tugging at Blackie's collar. "Let's get away from here, Mandy!" But Blackie didn't want to move. James's face grew redder and redder as he tried to get Blackie to stand up.

In the end, Grandad bent down and lifted Blackie's bottom from the ground. Then he dug in his pocket and passed a couple of coins to Mandy. "Go and buy some ice cream," he said, his mouth close to Blackie's ears.

Ice cream! Blackie seemed to recognise

that. He looked up at James, then tugged at his lead.

"Thanks, Mr Hope," James called over his shoulder as he and Mandy hurried off with Blackie leading the way.

Mandy bought two ice creams from the van. Blackie started to whine when he saw them and looked pleadingly at James. "You don't deserve any," James told him. "But . . ." James pulled a doggy treat out of his pocket and put the *tiniest* bit of ice cream on it. "Just to let him think he's got one of his own," he explained to Mandy.

Mandy nodded. They knew dogs shouldn't have ice cream, but the speck James had given him wouldn't do any harm.

"Shall we go back to Animal Ark now?" suggested Mandy, when they'd finished eating. "I can't wait to ask Mum and Dad if we can look after Harvey."

Mrs Hope was sitting at the big, pine table doing some paperwork when Mandy,

James and Blackie burst into the kitchen.

"We've thought of a brilliant name for the gerbil, Mum!" Mandy announced.

Mandy's mum agreed that Harvey was a good name, then she looked closely at Mandy's face. "I recognise that expression, Mandy Hope!" she said. "And what *else* have you thought of?"

Mandy rubbed one foot against the ankle of her other foot. "I know we won't be able to *keep* Harvey, Mum, but please could James and I look after him while he is here?"

"We mean clean out his cage and everything, Mrs Hope," said James, shoving his glasses back on to the bridge of his nose.

Mandy said they knew it would mean a lot of hard work and they'd have to be very patient with Harvey. "He'll be frightened of us for a while, so we'll have to talk to him a lot so he gets to know us and trust us. And I know we'd have to *learn* exactly how to look after him,

Mum. But we'd read up on that, wouldn't we, James?"

Mr Hope's deep laugh sounded from the doorway. He had a couple of slim books and some leaflets in one hand. He held them up and waved them at Mandy and James. Blackie woofed and darted over to say "hello". He was very fond of Mandy's dad.

"Whoa there, young fella! These aren't for you," said Adam Hope. Blackie was leaping up, trying to reach the books. "They're for Mandy and James."

"For us, Dad?" Mandy hurried to take them from him.

"From the surgery," he explained.

Mandy glanced down at them, then she flung her arms around her dad's waist. "How did you know?" she asked. "How did you know what we were talking about?"

"Magic," he teased, ruffling her hair. Blackie gave another woof and jumped up again.

"Both of you at once is just too much!"
Mr Hope protested.

Mandy moved away and thrust the
books and leaflets into her friend's hands
with a huge smile. They were all about
caring for gerbils: feeding them, taming
them, keeping them healthy . . .

"Wow!" said James, grinning back at
Mandy.

Emily Hope smiled. "We already
guessed you'd ask to look after him," she
said. "But," she added, "you'll have to
wait until he starts recovering."

"That'll give us time to read the books
and leaflets, won't it, James?"

"From cover to cover," he said.

"I've put a card on the surgery notice-
board asking if anyone has lost a gerbil,"
said Mr Hope.

"And we'll put one on the school
bulletin board," said James.

"That's a good idea," Mr Hope said.
"But if nobody's claimed him in a week
or so . . ." he looked meaningfully at

Mandy, ". . . we'll have to start looking for a good home for him."

Mandy met his gaze and nodded. She didn't like thinking about that, but at least they'd have Harvey for a little while.

James had wandered to the kitchen table and was sitting with his head propped in his hands. He was reading one of the leaflets already. Mandy dragged a chair round so she could sit next to him. She reached out for one of the books and opened it.

A few seconds later her mum said, "I thought I'd have the kitchen to myself for a while to do my paperwork. Suddenly there are two eager beavers at the table and one pest of a dog chewing at my laces!"

James jumped up looking really worried. Mandy giggled and pulled him back down. She knew her mum had only been teasing. "We want to make sure we know everything there is to know, Mum. While Harvey's here, he's going to be the best-looked-after gerbil ever!"

6

Spreading the news

Next morning there was no sign of James when Mandy arrived at the huge old oak tree on the village green. They always met there to cycle the rest of the way to school together.

Mandy propped her bike against the tree and went over to the pond to look at the tadpoles. She knelt down and peered into the water.

The tadpoles were getting really big now: some of them had grown two tiny back legs. Mandy knew their front legs were growing as well, but they were hidden by little gill plates. When the gills disappeared she'd be able to see the front legs as well. And, soon after, the tadpoles' tails would get shorter and shorter . . . "Then," Mandy murmured, "you'll change into little froglets and be hopping all over the green!"

Mandy watched for a little while longer, then she heard someone calling her. She stood up and turned to see Paul Stevens propping his bike next to hers. Paul was eight, a year younger than her. He was in the same class as James, and lived in Jasmine Cottage, near Gran and Grandad.

"Hi, Paul," said Mandy, walking to meet him. "How's Paddy?" Paddy was Paul's Exmoor pony.

"Fantastic!" Paul beamed. "We went

for a brilliant ride over the moors with the Pony Club yesterday. How's the gerbil? Your grandad told me about him last night. Did you really find him in one of our mouse houses?"

Mandy nodded, then told Paul the whole story. "I couldn't see him this morning. He's having his operation at nine o'clock and Mum didn't want him disturbed beforehand."

"He'll probably be wide awake and running round when you get home from school," said Paul.

"I hope so," said Mandy. "Then, tomorrow or the next day, James and I can start looking after him," she finished off happily.

"Let me know if you want any help," Paul offered. "You and James helped me a lot with Paddy when I first got him from the rescue sanctuary."

Mandy explained that because Harvey had been living wild he'd probably be nervous of humans for a while.

Paul nodded. "Do you think I could come and see him when he isn't frightened of people any more?"

"Of course you can, Paul," she replied.

The church clock chimed in the distance and Mandy sighed. "I don't know where James is, but we'd better go or we'll be late."

Welford Primary School was on Church Lane, a small lane off the upper high street at the side of the church.

James caught up with Paul and Mandy just as they were cycling past the church.

He was pedalling furiously and looked warm and out of breath.

"Mum says Harvey's doing fine," Mandy told him. "But why are you so late, James? Did you oversleep?"

"I forgot the mouse-count notebook," he replied breathlessly. "I had to go back for it."

The notebook was important. They were supposed to take it to Mrs Garvie, the Headteacher, before assembly. Mrs Garvie was going to tell the whole school the results of the first mouse-counting day.

"I almost forgot the notice for the bulletin board," Mandy admitted, as they rode towards the bike shed. She and James had written it yesterday before James had gone home.

Once they'd wheeled their bikes into the special racks, Mandy opened her schoolbag and pulled the notice out to show Paul. It had a drawing of a mouse house in the middle and around the drawing were the words:

Mandy Hope and James Hunter have
found a gerbil in a mouse house.
We are going to call him Harvey.
If anyone has lost a gerbil, please
contact Animal Ark.

"What will happen if you don't find
his owner?" Paul asked. "I shouldn't think
he belongs to anyone from school,
because *they*'d have put a notice on the
board saying they'd *lost* him."

Mandy told him her dad was putting a
notice up on Animal Ark's board, too.

"But if nobody claims him we'll have
to find him a good home," said James.
Then he looked up at the school building
and saw Mrs Garvie looking down at
them from her office window. "We'd
better hurry, Mandy. I think Mrs Garvie
is waiting for the notebook."

Paul said he'd pin the notice up
for them.

"Put it in the best place you can," Mandy
called, as she and James dashed off.

★ ★ ★

"I see you found twenty-eight mouse houses with the food gone from them?" Mrs Garvie said a short while later, as she looked at the mouse-counting notebook.

Mandy and James nodded.

"And we decided to count one harvest mouse for every three empty mouse houses. So, how many harvest mice can we say are living in or around the reedbeds?"

"At least nine, Mrs Garvie," said Mandy.

The Headteacher nodded and smiled. "I'll give out these details right after assembly. Then I'll send a report to all the other schools taking part in the survey. And I should be hearing from them soon, with details of *their* first mouse counts."

Mandy and James looked at each other. Should they tell Mrs Garvie about Harvey? She might not see the bulletin board until *after* she'd sent her report to all the other schools, and they might be interested to know what they'd found in one of the mouse houses.

"Is there something else?" Mrs Garvie asked.

Then Mandy and James told her all about it: from when Grandad had heard something inside the mouse house, right up to why they'd decided to call the gerbil Harvey.

"Goodness me," said Mrs Garvie. "I think I'll have to make a special announcement about this after the mouse-count report. Or better still, how about you two coming up on the platform and telling everyone yourselves?"

"We made a notice for the bulletin board and Paul Stevens is pinning it up for us right now," James said in alarm. He didn't fancy standing up in front of the whole school!

"But we haven't put much information on it, James," said Mandy. "I could do it on my own if you like."

Mandy crossed her fingers while she waited for James's reply. She didn't *really* want to go up on to the platform on her own.

"No, it's OK, I'll do it with you," James said.

Mandy smiled happily at Mrs Garvie. She'd known James wouldn't let her down.

When the time came during assembly for Mandy and James to go up on to the platform, James felt nervous all over again. But once Mandy had started talking, he joined in eagerly. He even asked if anyone had lost a gerbil matching Harvey's description.

But nobody had lost a gerbil. And everybody wondered where Harvey had lived before he'd found his way into one of their mouse houses.

Then Pam Stanton waved her hand in the air. She asked Mrs Garvie if the school could have a Harvey announcement every day. "He *was* found in one of *our* mouse houses," she pointed out.

Mrs Garvie thought every day would be a bit too much, but she said James and Mandy could give the school an update once a week.

"And," said Mandy to James at break, "we should have plenty to tell everyone next week. By then, we'll have spent four or five days looking after Harvey. Oh," she added, hugging herself with excitement. "I just can't wait for Mum to tell us we can start!"

7

Making friends

After school, James and Mandy rode quickly to Animal Ark. Maybe they'd be able to see Harvey for a few minutes!

"That's if he's all right," said Mandy. She'd been worrying all day.

"I'm sure he will be," James tried to reassure her.

"I wonder if he'll be able to eat yet?" said Mandy, as they wheeled their bikes up the garden path. "If we knew what his favourite food was, we could have put some in his cage to show him we're friends."

"What treats do Terry and Jerry like best?" James wondered. Terry and Jerry were Class 5's gerbils – Mandy and the rest of her class all helped look after them.

"Terry likes raisins and Jerry *loves* a little bit of tomato," Mandy replied.

"Well, Harvey might like both of those," said James. "Let's ask your mum if it would be OK to give him some of each."

"Good idea," said Mandy. "Let's go and find her."

Mrs Hope was just coming out of the unit when Mandy and James hurried into the surgery. "Harvey's fine," she told Mandy, before she had time to ask.

Mandy ran to hug her. "I knew he *would* be OK, Mum," she said. "But I just couldn't help worrying."

"You can have five minutes with him," said Mrs Hope. Her green eyes twinkled when she saw their excited faces.

Then Mandy's words tumbled out quickly as she told her mum what she and James had thought of. ". . . So do you think it would be all right to give Harvey a couple of raisins and a small piece of tomato?"

"I think it's a very good idea," said Mrs Hope. "But remember to move your hands very slowly when you're putting anything in the cage."

"So we don't frighten him," added James.

"That's right," said Mrs Hope. "And it's a bit soon to try and get him to take anything from your fingers yet. I think you'd better just put his treats near his food dish."

"I hope Harvey will like them," said Mandy.

"Me, too." Her mum smiled. "It might stop him from chewing the wood chips off the floor of his cage and throwing the bits out through the bars!"

"Is that what he's been doing?" Mandy asked.

Mrs Hope nodded. "I think Harvey might be feeling a little bored. I've put a couple of cardboard tubes in his cage, but I think he needs something more interesting to play with," she told them. "I'm sure I can leave that to you two, though."

"You bet!" said James, edging to one side and trying to peer into the unit.

"In you go, the pair of you." Mrs Hope laughed. "You can look at Harvey while I fetch his treats."

Mandy followed James into the unit and over to Harvey's cage. But to their disappointment, there was no sign of the gerbil. Mandy thought he must be in his wooden nesting-box at the back of the cage, then James suddenly pointed to one of the cardboard tubes.

The lower half of Harvey's face was

300

peeping out of one end. His whiskers were twitching and he was staring at them, his eyes round and dark and curious.

"Let's crouch down and put our faces quite close to the cage," Mandy suggested quietly.

James nodded and, moving together, they slowly and silently bent down.

A little scratching sound came from the tube – Harvey's claws were moving inside. For a moment it seemed as though he was going to wriggle backwards and hide away. Mandy and James froze, hardly daring to breathe. But Harvey stayed where he was.

"I think it would be OK for us to talk around him," Mandy murmured. "To get him used to the sound of our voices." She breathed excitedly as Harvey's front feet crept a little way out of the tube. The rest of his face began to appear. Mandy smiled as his ears, which must have been flattened against the inside of the tube, suddenly popped up.

"Hello, Harvey," Mandy said softly. "We won't hurt you. We want to make friends."

James told Harvey he was a very brave gerbil.

Harvey stared solemnly back. Mandy was sure he was waiting for one of them to speak again.

Just then the unit door opened. Harvey scrabbled his feet, gave a frightened squeak and, quick as a flash, withdrew his head and moved right back inside the tube.

Mandy and James stood up and Simon, who'd recently come to work at Animal Ark, walked towards them. He was holding a saucer containing a piece of tomato and two raisins. Simon wasn't a vet, he was a nurse. He helped with operations and looked after animals who had to stay for a while. He kept them clean and comfortable, soothed the creatures and talked to them, changed their dressings, fed them and gave them any medicine they needed.

The two friends liked Simon. He was always willing to answer their questions about animals and he knew quite a lot about wildlife as well as pets.

"Your mum's been called out," Simon explained to Mandy. "She asked me to bring this in for you to give to the gerbil. She also reminded you not to stay in here too long."

"We'll put Harvey's treats in the cage, then watch for a very *little* while to see if he comes out," said Mandy. "Will you wait with us, Simon?"

"OK," he said. "But that doesn't mean you can spend any more time with Harvey!"

Mandy smiled, then passed James the piece of tomato. He put it carefully into the cage and Mandy put the raisins next to it.

The three of them stepped back and waited. But not even a whisker appeared from the tube. "Come on," said Simon. "He'll probably pop out and gobble everything up as soon as we've gone."

"He let us look at him and talk to him for a while, Simon," Mandy said, as she closed the unit door behind them. "But he didn't come right out of the tube, so we couldn't see his tail end."

"He's still got a bit of a tail," Simon told her. "About this much, I'd say," he added, holding his thumb and forefinger about two and a half centimetres apart.

"Maybe he'll let us see *all* of him next time," said James.

Simon nodded. "Gerbils are curious and nosy little creatures," he said. "In time, wanting to know and see what's going on makes them forget their fear."

"Mrs Hope said he needs something interesting to play with," said James. "If we could think of something to put in his cage tomorrow, do you think he'd feel curious enough to go and look at it?"

Simon thought it was a good idea. Now all Mandy and James needed to do was to find something really exciting to make for Harvey.

"Phone your mum and ask if you can stay for tea, James," Mandy suggested. She knew her parents wouldn't mind – James was always welcome at Animal Ark.

"OK," James agreed. "Then we can have a good think."

"Remember how we made an adventure playground for Frisky?" said James as he and Mandy laid the table for tea. "Well, perhaps we could do something like that for Harvey."

Frisky was a small Russian hamster who'd once stayed with Mandy's grandparents while his owner was on holiday. Mandy and James had helped look after him for a whole week and they'd made his cage a really exciting play place for him.

"I read in one of those books Dad gave us that gerbils tend to be even more adventurous than hamsters," said Mandy. "We'll have to think of all sorts of things he can wriggle into and climb up. Maybe we could make him a maze out of little cardboard boxes with holes in the top."

"We could leave one or two boxes open and put a little ladder or a thick branch in. Then he'll be able to climb up and down and in and out of them," said James.

"Sounds like gerbil talk to me," said a voice from the doorway.

It was Mr Hope. He came in and put a narrow box with rounded ends on the table. "Nuts and raisins for you," he told Mandy. "Mrs Edwards sent them. I've just been to check Tilly's puppies."

Mrs Edwards had a greengrocery shop and Tilly was her Corgi.

"How many puppies did she have, Dad? Are they OK?"

Adam Hope smiled. "She had two. Mum and pups are doing fine. The puppies are both boys and they look just like their dad."

"Isn't their dad a Corgi, too?" Mandy asked.

"No!" Mr Hope's eyes twinkled. "Their dad is Mike Jordan's Arnie."

Mandy laughed. "We'd better not tell Arnie about his sons. He'll want to take them home and put them in his basket."

James hadn't said a word. Mandy wondered why, and turned to look at him. He was staring hard at the box of nuts and raisins. "You can have some after tea if you like," Mandy told him.

Her friend shook his head. "It's not them. It's the box they're in," he explained. "I've thought of exactly the right thing to make for Harvey."

8

Gerbil jinks

Mandy was so curious about James's idea she couldn't eat her tea fast enough. She finished long before her friend did and then had to wait for him!

She kept looking at the box, but she just couldn't guess what James had in mind for it.

James finished at last and Mandy jumped up to clear the table. Then she took the lid off the box and tipped the nuts and raisins into a small bowl. James reached for a nut and nibbled it as he gazed thoughtfully at the box.

"We need quite a small, square or oblong box that will fit inside this one at one end," he said. "And some smaller boxes as well . . . and the inside of a kitchen roll to cut down for a funnel and—"

"I get it!" Mandy interrupted excitedly. "We're going to turn the box into a boat!"

"Yes!" James grinned up at her. "A cargo boat!"

"And the cargo will be food," said Mandy. "We've got some of it already. We can hide some of the raisins or pieces of carrot or turnip or a grape inside the little boxes. Oh, it's a brilliant idea, James! Mum and Dad are bound to have cardboard tubes and little boxes in the surgery."

The cargo boat soon took shape. James

carefully cut two holes in the box they were using for the bridge area: one hole for a door and the other to push the funnel into. Mandy cut holes in the smaller boxes and arranged them at the other end of the boat in a sort of maze.

"If Harvey likes his cargo boat, we can keep adding things to it," Mandy said happily.

"Mmm." James nodded. "A ladder would be good, wouldn't it? We could stand the boat on a block of wood or another box, so he'd have to climb up the ladder to get on to it."

Mandy decided a box would be better than a block of wood. "Because then," she said, "we can make *another* play area inside the box, and it will be—"

"A multistorey play area!" James finished the sentence for her. "Wow!" he added. "I can't wait for tomorrow."

At school next day, Mrs Garvie read out the reports from some of the other schools taking part in the harvest mouse survey. One school said that none of the food had gone from the tennis-ball mouse houses, and two other schools reported quite a high success rate.

"But nobody else found a gerbil in a mouse house!" added Carrie Anderson, who was in Mandy's class. "I've got something for Harvey," she said and she handed Mandy a small wooden ball. "I bought it for Bingo, my budgie," Carrie told her. "He doesn't play with it so I thought Harvey might like it."

"That's great, Carrie. Thanks," said Mandy.

When Mandy went to find James at playtime, he showed her a wooden brick with two holes in it.

"I brought it for Harvey," said Amy Fenton. "It's one especially for pets. Someone bought it for Minnie but she's already got lots of playthings." Minnie was Amy's white mouse.

Mandy smiled. "Tell Minnie thank

you," she said. Then she showed James and Amy the little wooden ball Carrie had given her.

It wasn't Mandy's turn to feed Terry and Jerry, the class gerbils, but she watched Richard Tanner and Jill Redfern while they did it. She wanted to see what the gerbils liked best after raisins and tomato.

"I always bring Terry a small piece of parsley when it's my turn to feed him," said Jill.

"And Jerry likes sunflower seeds," said Richard, laughing as the gerbil scurried over and climbed into his hand to nibble the seed.

Mandy longed for the day when Harvey would be tame enough to do that!

"I know we've got to be patient," she said to James as they rode home from school. "But it'll be so nice when Harvey starts to trust us!"

When they hurried into the surgery, Mr Hope greeted them with a smile. "I'm sure Harvey is waiting for you," he said. "He's had his nose pressed to the cage bars for the last ten minutes."

"Does he look all right?" Mandy asked. She felt a tiny bit worried about seeing him with just a tiny tail.

"He looks great," Mr Hope assured her.

As soon as they went into the unit, Harvey started squeaking. Mandy beamed at James and they walked slowly towards the cage, talking in low voices.

They got closer and closer to the cage. Harvey squeaked again, then rose up on his hind legs and gripped the cage bars with his front claws.

"This is a nice welcome," said Mandy, crouching down slowly. "And Dad's right. He looks great, James. His tiny tail doesn't make him look strange at all."

"He's got such a cute face, you don't really notice his tail's shorter than it should be," agreed James.

Harvey hadn't moved away from the cage bars, so James crouched down as

well. "Hello, Harvey," he said. "We've made you something to play with. We'll go and get it in a minute or two. Then we'll bring you some treats to nibble. After that, we'll feed you and give you some fresh water."

Harvey moved his head to one side and stared at James.

"I think he's starting to like us talking to him," Mandy said. Harvey turned his head slightly and looked at her.

Then, very, very slowly, Mandy walked her fingers up the cage bars until they were close to Harvey's front paws. The gerbil pulled his body back a little way when she ran the tip of one finger over his curled claws, but he didn't take his paw away.

"See if he'll let you stroke his tummy, Mandy," said James.

"OK," breathed Mandy, slowly moving her fingers down the bars. "Here goes."

Mandy stroked the soft, pale-gold fur four times before Harvey decided he'd been brave enough! He moved away quickly with a little squeak and disappeared inside a cardboard tube.

Feeling happy and excited, Mandy and James went to find Mr Hope to tell him all about it.

"That's really good progress," he said, smiling at them.

Mandy nodded. "And now we're going to fetch his cargo boat and some little treats to hide in the boxes. Do you think it would be OK to give him some sunflower seeds, Dad?"

"Just one or two," he said, going on to explain that too many sunflower seeds could cause skin problems for a gerbil.

Mandy said they'd only hide one sunflower seed to be on the safe side.

When they went into the kitchen, Mrs Hope was preparing tea. "It's salad," she said. "I'm preparing it now, so it will be ready to eat as soon as surgery's over."

Mandy and James told her all about Harvey, too, and they showed her the wooden ball and the brick with holes in it.

"That was nice of Carrie and Amy," said Mrs Hope. "But you'd better wash them in mild disinfectant and let them dry before you give them to Harvey — just to make sure there aren't any germs on them."

"We'll do that after we've given him this," said Mandy, reaching for the cargo boat she'd tucked away in a safe corner. "He can have them tomorrow."

James was watching Mrs Hope grate some cheese. She smiled and handed him a piece.

"Gerbils like cheese, don't they?" Mandy said. "I read it in one of the pamphlets."

"OK, you can cut a small piece for him," her mum said.

"So we'll hide cheese, a sunflower seed and . . . and, what else, James?"

"Carrot?" suggested James, pointing to the bowl of salad.

"There'll be nothing left for us to eat at

this rate," Mrs Hope teased as she lifted a small teaspoonful of grated carrot from the bowl.

When they'd hidden the food in three of the boxes in the little maze, they hurried through to the surgery and into the unit.

James opened Harvey's cage and carefully slid the cargo boat in. "Look, Mandy, he's watching from inside the tube," he said.

And, almost before James had closed the cage door, Harvey was scampering eagerly towards his new plaything. He ran all round the outside of it, sniffing and squeaking to himself. Then he climbed inside and went through the round door of the box that had the kitchen roll funnel sticking up through its top.

They could hear him moving around, then Mandy gave a little gasp and pointed to the funnel. It was slowly rising upwards.

"He must be pushing the end that's inside the box with his head!" said James.

"Isn't he clever? He's making up a game of his own!"

Harvey pushed the kitchen roll all the way out and the next minute he popped up through the hole where it had been. He sat on the top of the box for a couple of seconds, his nose and whiskers twitching.

"It looks as if he can still balance all right," said James.

"He's wobbling a little bit," said Mandy, "but not much!" Then she smiled as Harvey jumped down. He ran to the other end of the boat to the maze she'd made with the small boxes.

He's going to the one where I've hidden the cheese! thought Mandy, watching with big, round eyes.

Harvey carried the little square of cheese out, jumped over the side of the boat and put the cheese down in the middle of his cage. Then he climbed back on to the boat and into the maze. This time he made straight for the box where the sunflower seed was hidden.

Mandy and James listened carefully, then grinned at each other. They could hear the gerbil munching at it.

"I wonder if he'll find the carrot next," said Mandy.

Harvey went into the box with the carrot in, but he came out quickly, jumped over the side again and made his way to the piece of cheese. He ate about half of it, then sat on his haunches and rubbed his paws over his face. He was cleaning himself!

He cleaned his eyes, his ears, his nose and his mouth, then he lowered his front legs to the ground and ran into his nesting-box.

"Wow!" said James. "He had a really good time."

"I think he's starting to get quite tame already," said Mandy. "I'm sure he kept checking to see if we were watching when he was playing on his boat."

Mandy gave a small sigh as they went out of the unit. The quicker Harvey became tame, the quicker they'd have to try to find a home for him!

Mr Jordan was in the waiting-room with Arnie, so Mandy and James went to say hello.

"What's wrong with Arnie?" Mandy asked, bending down to stroke him.

"He decided he wanted to look after next door's kitten," said Mr Jordan. "He popped it through the cat-flap, then tried to get in after it and got stuck!" Mike Jordan hadn't got a cat. But Mandy knew he lived in the house in Meadow Lane where the Greenes used to live. They'd

probably put the cat-flap in the door for their cat.

She was called Tibby and she'd had six kittens just before the Greenes had moved. Mandy had found them all a home at Westmoor House, an old people's nursing home a couple of kilometres away.

"I had to give Arnie a good hard tug to get him out," Mr Jordan explained. "The poor little chap yelped quite hard. I think he's only a bit bruised, but we're going on holiday tomorrow so I'm getting him checked just to be sure."

While Mandy and James petted Arnie, Mike Jordan asked how the gerbil was. He'd heard all about him from Mandy's gran.

"He's brilliant!" said James. "You should have seen him playing on the boat we made for him. He's really clever, isn't he, Mandy?"

Mandy nodded and felt a bit sad again. "We'll need to find him a home soon," she said, looking hopefully up at Mr Jordan. It would be great if Harvey could stay in Welford, then she and James would be able to visit him.

Mr Jordan shook his head. "I couldn't chance having a gerbil," he said. "Arnie would be sure to want to pick him up and carry him around. And *we* know he wouldn't hurt him, but . . ."

Mandy nodded. "But Harvey wouldn't know that," she agreed. "He'd be frightened."

"Don't worry, Mandy," said James, as he got ready to go. "Harvey's going to turn into a really fantastic pet. I'm sure we'll be able to find him a good home when the time comes."

9

A brilliant idea

By the time the weekend came, Mandy and James weren't feeling quite so confident about Harvey. True, he always seemed to be waiting for them when they hurried to see him after school. He looked at them when they talked to him and he let them stroke him through the cage bars.

But he still ran and hid in a tube or in his nesting-box whenever they put anything in the cage or when they gave him fresh food and water.

And, although he played all sorts of games in, on and around the boxes on the cargo boat, he hadn't taken any notice at all of the wooden ball or the brick. Grandad had brought a tiny terracotta plant-pot round, but Harvey ignored that as well.

On Saturday morning, Harvey wouldn't even come to the front of the cage when Mandy called him. He poked his head out of his nesting-box, but that was all.

"I don't think he's ill," she said to James. "He's eaten quite a lot of the food we gave him yesterday afternoon and his eyes are nice and bright."

"He just seems to have gone back to being nervous." James sighed. "Let's go away for a little while. He might be OK when we come back."

When they went back a couple of hours later, Harvey was standing up at the cage bars. But he ran off when Mandy tried to stroke his tummy.

Mandy and James mentioned the problem to Simon, and he suggested Mandy made a play area for Harvey.

"Your hands might not seem so big and threatening inside a larger space," he said. "And he might play with more things if he had more room to play in. There are quite a few tall cardboard boxes waiting to be collected for recycling. You could use them as a barrier."

"We could put his cage inside the area and leave the door open," suggested Mandy. "And if Harvey comes out we can take his cage away and clean it out. It's a brilliant idea. Thanks, Simon!"

Mrs Hope said they could make a play area in the kitchen as long as they protected the floor with cardboard and paper. "And," she advised, "when you take his cage away, take the nesting-box out of it and put it in the play area. Then Harvey will know he's got somewhere safe to run to."

While Mandy was fetching the tall cardboard boxes, James went to get something from the saddlebag on his bike.

"Apple-tree twigs and cotton string," he said to Mandy. "I thought we could have a go at making a ladder."

Twenty minutes later, Harvey emerged cautiously through his cage door. He wiggled his nose and twitched his whiskers then scurried towards the cargo boat. Mandy had put it on top of another box, and James had put the twig ladder at the end where the maze was. On top of one of the tiny boxes was a special gerbil chocolate drop.

In no time at all Harvey climbed up the ladder. Squeaking excitedly, he sniffed at the chocolate drop before eating it. Then he sat up on his haunches as if to say, "What's next?"

Mandy leaned over very slowly, lifted the cage out and passed it to her friend. James removed the nesting-box. Then, resting it on his up-turned palms, he lowered it carefully into one corner of Harvey's play area.

"Keep your hands under it, James," said Mandy. "Harvey's watching, aren't you, boy?"

Harvey popped into the nesting-box, then popped out again – scampering over James's fingers both times.

Mandy tiptoed to the kitchen table and got another chocolate drop. Then she stuck it between two of James's fingertips. She didn't have time to move away before Harvey darted over to nibble at the chocolate treat. And when he'd finished it, he sniffed at Mandy's hand.

"I haven't got any," she told him. "How about a little stroke instead?"

Harvey didn't move, so Mandy stroked him under the chin with one finger. He stared solemnly up at her as she stroked

him, talking softly all the time.

After a while, Harvey squeaked and moved away.

"He's sniffing at the wooden ball," said James. "He's . . . Oh, wow, Mandy!"

They stared in delight as Harvey pushed the ball with his nose, ran after it and pushed it again. "He's playing football," said Mandy.

James leaned over one of the tall boxes and held his hands in a butterfly shape. "Nose the ball to me, Harvey," he said.

Harvey blinked. Then he nosed the ball hard and sent it straight into James's hands. "Goal!" James laughed.

"That was just luck," said Mandy. "He couldn't really have understood."

But James carefully rolled the ball back to the gerbil. "To me, Harvey," he said. And Harvey nosed it back.

"He's a genius!" said Mandy after Harvey had 'scored' five goals. "A *gerbil genius!*"

She picked up the ball, made a cup shape with her hand and rested it on the floor.

Harvey scampered over and hopped into her hand. Mandy held her breath and wondered if she dared to try putting her other hand over the top of Harvey's body.

"Go on," said James, when she glanced at him.

"It's OK, Harvey," she murmured. "I won't squash you. What a brave boy." She was holding Harvey. She was holding him at last!

After a few seconds, Mandy raised her hands carefully, keeping them close to her body with Harvey facing towards her. And he didn't seem to mind at all!

"I think he likes it!" said James. He'd moved to stand as close as he could. "Look, he's put his face out. He's sniffing at your T-shirt."

Mandy lowered her face and rubbed her nose against Harvey's. And when Harvey looked at her with his big, dark, chocolate-brown eyes, Mandy felt happy and sad at the same time. Harvey was beginning to trust them at last. But now,

they'd really have to start trying to find a home for him!

On Monday morning Mandy and James talked the problem over with some of their classmates. They were making their way down to the reedbeds to carry out another mouse count.

There wouldn't be many more mouse counts after this. They knew now that there were harvest mice living near the reeds in Welford – and the reports from the other schools taking part in the survey showed which other areas were home to them as well.

"And even if Welford hasn't got the *most* harvest mice, our results will be the most unusual because we found Harvey in one of our mouse houses!" said Mandy.

She and James had given a "Harvey update" after assembly, so everyone knew the gerbil was doing well. Since nobody had claimed him, he was now nearly ready to go to a new home.

"Gerbils are happier when they've got another gerbil to play with," said Mandy. "Like Terry and Jerry. But it says in one of my books that they should be introduced to each other before they're eight weeks old or they'll fight. Mum thinks Harvey's five or six months old."

"That means finding somewhere special for him," James said. "He'll need a home where there's someone to play football with him and teach him more games. He's *so* clever; he just loves learning things!"

They'd reached the mouse houses by now and, to Mandy's surprise, James didn't seem to be very interested in what they were doing.

"Are you OK?" she asked, after a while.

James nodded. "Just thinking," he said. Then suddenly he stopped dead. "Listen!" he said. "I've got a brilliant idea. I don't know *how* we didn't think of it before!"

Everyone else stopped whatever they were in the middle of doing with the tennis-ball mouse houses and looked at James. They could tell he was excited.

"Wouldn't Class 4 be the perfect place for Harvey? We haven't got a class pet," said James.

"Let's ask Mrs Black about it right now!" said Amy Fenton.

"Yes," said Paul. "It is a brilliant idea, James!"

"No, don't ask yet," Mandy said urgently. "When I was in Class 4, I asked Mrs Black if we could have a class pet."

"I remember that," said Pam Stanton.

"She said she'd never have another class pet because the last time she'd allowed her class to have a hamster she'd ended up looking after it herself."

Mandy nodded. "And she could never find anyone to take it home for the school holidays, so she had to do that, too!"

"Well, I couldn't have Harvey for the holidays because of Benji," James admitted gloomily. Benji was James's cat. "Maybe it wasn't such a good idea after all."

"It was, James," said Mandy. "There must be others who could have Harvey for the holidays."

"I'm sure I'd be able to," said Paul.

"And me," added Amy.

"We just need to think up a way to convince Mrs Black that there'd always be someone to look after Harvey at school *and* at home," said Mandy.

"She's coming over," whispered Amy. "Let's talk about it when we get back to school."

10

Making plans

That day there were forty mouse houses without any seed left in them. Mrs Todd and Mrs Black couldn't understand why their pupils didn't seem more excited – or why they seemed so eager to get back to school!

Mandy and her friends *were* pleased to

know that even more harvest mice seemed to be using the special feeding houses. But somehow, making plans for Harvey to be Class 4's pet seemed much more important.

During lunch-break they all went into a little huddle in a corner of the playground.

Pam Stanton said she wished they'd got a photo of Harvey. "Then we could have shown it to Mrs Black and said what a shame it was that such a beautiful gerbil hadn't got a home to go to," she said.

James looked at Paul. "You drew a great picture of Paddy," he said. "Could you come and see Harvey after school and draw a picture of him?"

Paul nodded. "You bet!" he said.

Mandy's eyes sparkled. "We could make the drawing into a card. A card with some rhymes inside."

"Rhymes about a gerbil looking for a home," said Pam.

"A home where there are lots of children – somewhere he could learn things because he loves learning!" added Amy.

"And we should have a rhyme about how well *we'd* look after him," said James. "We can leave the card on Mrs Black's desk with a bunch of flowers!" said Tina Cunningham. "I'm sure Dad will let me pick some out of the garden."

They spent the last playtime of the day coming up with rhymes. Mandy said she'd take them home. She and James could stick them on to a piece of card while Paul was drawing his picture of Harvey.

"Mrs Black always goes straight into the classroom when she arrives," said Mandy. "If we all get here a few minutes early tomorrow, we can put the flowers and the card on her desk."

"Then we can peep through the window and watch her face when she reads the card," said James.

Everything went to plan next morning. Mandy and James had stuck all the rhymes on the inside of a piece of folded card and Paul had stuck his drawing of Harvey on the outside. It was a really good drawing of him standing up against the bars of his cage. Paul had drawn a speech bubble coming from the gerbil's mouth. Inside it he'd written: *Please let me come to school and be Class 4's pet!*

Tina Cunningham had brought a small posy of garden flowers wrapped in paper, tied with a ribbon. Mr Simpson, the school caretaker, had allowed James to go into the classroom to put the card and flowers on Mrs Black's desk.

Now, they were all looking in at the window, watching Mrs Black.

"She's smiling," Mandy whispered.

"I bet she's looking at my rhyme," said James. "It wasn't a very good one."

" 'This gerbil genius, will be very keen on us . . . if we have him in Class 4. He'll behave very well and listen and learn . . . because that's what classrooms are for!' " Mandy quoted James's rhyme with a giggle.

"Mine was worse than that!" Pam laughed. " 'Harvey the gerbil is feeling blue. Mrs Black's got a heart of gold. If she'd allow Harvey to come to school too, we'd look after him without being told!' "

"I didn't know that was your rhyme." Mandy giggled. "You're right, Pam, it *is* worse than James's."

Just then, Paul gave a little gasp. Mrs Black was coming over to the window.

"And what about school holidays?" she

asked, popping her head out. "Who'll look after him then?"

Tina, Paul and Amy dug into their backpacks and each pulled out a letter. "We thought of that, Mrs Black!" said Amy. "These are from our parents saying we can take Harvey home in the holidays."

"We can take it in turns," said Paul.

"And what's he going to live in?" asked Mrs Black.

They all looked at each other in dismay. They hadn't thought of that.

But then Mandy smiled. "I'm sure Mum and Dad would let us borrow a cage from Animal Ark for a while," she said.

"While we all save up our pocket money to buy him a cage of his own," Paul added. The others nodded.

"Very well," said Mrs Black. "I'll have a word with Mrs Garvie during morning break. *If* she agrees, I'll agree to a . . ." she held up a hand as everyone cheered, ". . . to a trial period," she said. "But if

Harvey stops you from concentrating on your lessons, or if I think he isn't being properly looked after—"

"We'll make a list like Class 5's got for looking after Terry and Jerry," said James. "We'll all take it in turns to do the important things, like feeding him and changing his water and cleaning him out."

"And when you let us choose a reward for finishing our work early, we could choose to play with Harvey," said Tina.

The lining-up bell rang just then. They all sped away and got into line, standing straight and quiet! They were all silently wishing hard for Mrs Garvie to say yes.

The first part of the morning seemed to go really slowly. And, for once, when playtime came, everybody wanted it to end quickly!

Then they wanted it to last a bit longer, because Mrs Black came into the playground to tell them that Mrs Garvie had agreed to let them have Harvey for a trial period of two weeks!

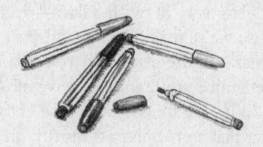

11

Harvey on trial

"You'll never guess what Harvey does now!" Mandy said excitedly to her mum and Simon one day after school.

It was almost two weeks since Mrs Hope had driven Mandy to school with Harvey in the cage loaned from Animal Ark. Every day Mandy came home and told her parents and Simon what the gerbil had been up to.

"Well, every time the bell for playtime rings, he squeaks and runs up his ladder! Our class was in with Class 4 today, because we're making a huge map so we can mark off the places where we know harvest mice are living. And we all saw him do it. We think it's because Harvey knows that someone puts his toys in his cage when the bell rings, so he can have a playtime as well!"

"I expect he'd run up his ladder and squeak if he heard a whistle or some other noise," said Simon.

"Do you think so?" Mandy looked disappointed. "I'll ask Mrs Black if we can try him with other noises tomorrow," she said.

When Mandy asked the next day, Mrs Black and Mandy's teacher, Mrs Todd, thought the experiment was a good idea. They decided that the two classes should try it out just before morning playtime.

The teachers had opened the dividing doors between the classrooms. The two classes were working together again on the big map, which they'd spread out on the floor.

A short while before the bell for play-time was due to go, the classes stopped their lesson and Mrs Black gave a good long blow on her playground whistle.

Harvey rose up on to his haunches and stood stock still. Mrs Black blew the whistle again: Harvey didn't move. Then Mrs Todd said that might be because everyone was kneeling on the floor, watching him. "You all start to get up when the bell goes," she pointed out. "I'll make the alarm on my travelling clock buzz and you go to your tables, shuffle papers and push your chairs back."

The alarm-clock buzzer sounded and everyone dashed to a table and pretended to be getting ready for break. But still Harvey didn't go to his ladder.

It was only when the real break bell went that Harvey dashed to his ladder and ran up it squeaking louder than ever.

"It seems there's no fooling Harvey," said Mrs Black, smiling. "He really is a most clever gerbil!"

When the others went out to play, Amy Fenton and James stayed behind. Today was one of the days to clean out Harvey's cage. On those days, instead of going to the staffroom, Mrs Black stayed in the classroom during morning playtime with whoever was meant to clean out the cage.

James went to get the special cardboard box with tall sides where they put Harvey while his cage was being cleaned, and Amy lifted the gerbil out. She was careful to hold him facing her body so he couldn't jump suddenly and land on the floor.

Harvey sat in her hand, twitching his nose as she talked to him. But the second James came and put the box on the floor, he gave a loud squeak.

"He's being clever again." Amy laughed

as she lowered Harvey into the box. "He *knows* there are lots of playthings in here."

"He'll start looking for his wooden ball in a minute," said James, as he went to the cage and started to remove the soiled wood chips from the bottom of it.

"I've hidden it under one of the small boxes," he added, glancing across at Mrs Black. "Harvey will sniff at all the boxes until he finds the right one. Then he'll lift it up with his nose and push it out of the way so he can get the ball."

"That's amazing!" Mrs Black chuckled

when Harvey did exactly as James had said he would. Then she turned as someone knocked on the classroom door. "That will be Mrs Garvie with my cup of coffee," she said.

"Did you hear that, Harvey?" Amy whispered as Mrs Black went to open the door. "Mrs Black said you were amazing! I'm sure she's going to let you stay."

"I heard that, Amy Fenton!" Mrs Black walked back over with her drink. Amy turned pink and her teacher smiled. "But I must admit you're all taking very good care of him," she added.

"And of his cage," she continued, as James went to the sink to scrub Harvey's food dish and water container.

A few minutes later, they heard the lining-up bell. "Gosh!" said James. "I haven't finished Harvey's cage yet." He threw a worried look towards Mrs Black.

"It's all right, James," she said. "Break started late because of our experiment.

I'll give you a few minutes at lunch-time to finish it off."

"Will he mind going into his cage when there aren't any wood chips on the floor?" Amy asked anxiously.

"Leave him in his box," said Mrs Black. "But," she warned as the others came in from the playground, "there'll be big trouble if anyone so much as looks towards the box. I want us to get all the areas marked out on the map this morning."

"I think Mrs Black might be carrying out a little experiment of her own," James whispered, when Mrs Black was right at the far end of the room, handing out coloured pens.

Amy nodded. "Seeing if we can behave when we know Harvey isn't in his cage."

It was so interesting finding the areas where all the other schools had carried out their surveys, and then drawing tiny pictures of tennis-ball mouse houses. Nobody looked up from the map at all.

"You're all doing really well," said Mrs Todd, kneeling down next to Mandy.

"I think we've just about finished," said Mandy. "We've written the names of the schools in as well as drawing mouse houses in the places each school put them. We can't write in how many harvest mice there are in each area until Mrs Garvie gets the last reports."

"But we can write in how many we think there are in Welford," said James. "We had our last mouse-counting day last week."

Mandy gasped and looked at Mrs Todd. "We haven't marked our school or the reedbeds on the map!" she said.

"I wondered when you'd realise that." Her teacher smiled.

"So," said Mrs Black, from where she was kneeling at the other side of the map, "who's going to be the first to find Welford?"

Everyone knelt closer over the big map. But suddenly there was a funny little scuffling noise. James jumped as he felt something brush past his leg and against the inside of his arm.

"Harvey!" he said in astonishment as the gerbil scampered on to the map. "Quick everyone! Move closer together so he can't escape!"

But Harvey didn't make any attempt to move off the map. Nose down, he ran back and forth and from side to side over it. Then suddenly he stopped. He rose up on to his haunches and stared round at everyone in turn, his brown eyes shining brightly.

"Well," Mrs Black said softly. "I think that settles it, doesn't it?"

"It's the first time he's disturbed us during a lesson, Mrs Black," pleaded Amy. "Please give him another chance."

"He must have managed to climb up the side of the box," said James. "If you'll give him another chance, we promise we'll never leave him in it again unless we're watching him!"

"And—" began Mandy. But she stopped when Mrs Black held a hand up for silence.

"You can't imagine that I wouldn't let Harvey stay after this!" she said. "Just look at him. Look at *where* he's sitting!"

"Oh!" said James, his eyes huge and round behind his glasses. "He's . . . he's sitting on Welford!" he stuttered.

"That's right." Mrs Black smiled.

"More than that," said Mrs Todd. "He's sitting exactly on top of where we want to mark Welford Primary School."

Mrs Black nodded and leaned forward to pick Harvey up. "You're a gerbil genius," she told him. "We couldn't possibly let you go anywhere else now. You've shown us that Welford Primary School is where you belong!"

Everyone cheered as Mrs Black stood up and carried Harvey towards his cage.

"James! Amy!" she said over the cheers. "What are you waiting for? Come here and make Harvey's cage ready for him."

"Yes, Mrs Black," James and Amy laughed as they leaped to their feet and hurried to do just that.

Read more about Animal Ark in
Hamster Hotel

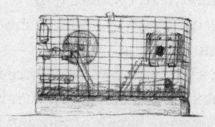

1

A visitor at Lilac Cottage

"Mandy Hope, did you hear what I said?" Mrs Todd was standing right beside Mandy's school desk.

Mandy looked up at her teacher. She had been miles away. Today was the day that her grandmother's friend Mary was bringing her hamster to stay at Lilac

357

Cottage, the house where Gran lived.

Mandy's grandparents were going to look after the hamster for a week while Mary was away on holiday and Mandy just couldn't wait to meet him.

"Oh, sorry, Mrs Todd," she said. "Er . . . no I didn't."

"What's the heaviest land animal in the world, next to the elephant, Mandy?"

The class were having a quiz and it was Mandy's turn to answer a question.

"Oh," Mandy said. "A rhinoceros."

You could ask Mandy anything about animals and she almost always knew the answer.

Mrs Todd nodded. "Good. Well done, Mandy!"

Mandy glanced up at the clock. Nearly three o'clock. Almost time to go home. Better still, it was half-term. She and her best friend, James Hunter, would have a whole week to spend with the hamster. James was a year younger than Mandy and loved animals almost as much as she did.

James had two pets. A Labrador puppy named Blackie and a cat called Benji. Mandy would have loved to have a pet too, but her parents were both vets and were too busy looking after other people's animals to have pets of their own.

Mandy wanted to be a vet like her parents one day. She longed to help out with the sick animals at their surgery, Animal Ark, but knew she would have to wait until she was older.

When school had finished, Mandy helped Mrs Todd take Terry and Jerry, the class gerbils, out to her car. Mrs Todd was going to care for them at her house during the holiday.

Mandy said goodbye to Mrs Todd, then ran to meet James who was waiting by the school gate. They always went home together.

"Today's hamster day!" Mandy zipped up her coat against the cold wind.

James pushed his glasses on to the bridge

of his nose. "I hadn't forgotten," he said. "When can I come and see him?"

"Mum said I could go straight to Gran's after school," Mandy said. "You could come with me now if you like."

"Will your gran mind?" James asked.

"Of course she won't," said Mandy.

"Great!" said James, hurrying to keep up. "Let me just tell Mum where I'm going."

He ran on ahead to his house.

"Don't be long," Mandy called. "And better not bring Blackie this time – he might frighten the hamster."

James disappeared into his house.

Mandy waited for him by the front gate. Suddenly a black nose pushed the back door open and Blackie came scampering out. James followed soon after.

"Blackie!" James shouted. "Come back."

Blackie threw himself at Mandy, all big paws and wagging tail. Mandy laughed and gave him a cuddle. Blackie rolled over on his back with his legs in the air so Mandy could tickle his tummy.

James caught up with them and grabbed the puppy's collar. "Blackie, *when* will you learn to do as you're told?" He shook the puppy gently and scolded him. "He's learned to open the door," James explained to Mandy.

"So I see," she chuckled.

Blackie stood up and began licking her face. Mandy gave him another hug. "You're a very clever dog," she said.

"Yes, he is, but when is he going to behave?" said James.

"Never, by the looks of it." Mandy pushed Blackie gently away. "You'll have to take him to proper puppy training classes."

"Dad's already taken him," James told her as he hauled Blackie back into the house. "But he caused a riot."

Mandy chuckled. "A riot?"

"Yes. He ran off with the trainer's whistle, pinched the biscuits they were going to have at break time and got hold of a lady's scarf and tore it to bits. Dad won't take him again."

If you like *Animal Ark*® then you'll love *Animal Action*! Subscribe for just **£8** and you can look forward to six issues of *Animal Action* magazine, throughout the year. Each issue of *Animal Action* is bursting with animal news and features, competitions and fun and games! Plus, when you subscribe, you'll become a free Animal Action Club member too, so we'll send you a fab joining pack and FREE donkey notepad and pen!

To subscribe, simply complete the form below – a photocopy is fine – and send it with a cheque for £8 (made payable to RSPCA) to RSPCA Animal Action Club, Wilberforce Way, Southwater, Horsham, West Sussex RH13 9RS.

Don't delay, join today!

Name:
Address:
Postcode: Date of birth:
Signature of parent/guardian:

Data Protection Act: This information will be held on computer and used only by the RSPCA.

Please allow 28 days for delivery. **AACHOD07**